ARMY OF ONE

Army of One

stories

JANET SARBANES

OTIS BOOKS / SEISMICITY EDITIONS

The Graduate Writing program
Otis College of Art and Design
LOS ANGELES ● 2008

Book design and typesetting: Rebecca Chamlee

ISBN-3: 978-0-9796177-1-3
ISBN-10: 0-9796177-1-5

OTIS BOOKS / SEISMICITY EDITIONS
The Graduate Writing program
Otis College of Art and Design
9045 Lincoln Boulevard
Los Angeles, CA 90045

www.otis.edu
www.gw.otis.edu
seismicity@otis.edu

CONTENTS

1

DEAR AUNT SOPHIE

From: 2brnt2b2@yahoo.com
Subject: interview
Date: 11/3/03 9:24:02 PM Pacific Daylight Time
To: sofipappas@aol.com

Dear Aunt Sophie:
Hi! It's Alexa. This is my first email ever! I just set up an account and got your email from my mom's address book. Do you think I could interview you? Love, Alexa

Date: 11/10/03 6:34:01 PM Pacific Daylight Time

Dear Aunt Sophie:
I was wondering if you got my e-mail last week. I have to do an interview for Social Studies with a person I admire and I would really, really like to do it with you. Love, Alexa

To: 2brnt2b2@aol.com

Why do you admire me?

To: sofipappas@aol.com

Because you're a writer, and that's what I want to be.

Subject: first question

Dear Aunt Sophie:
I know you haven't said yes, but I'm going to send the first question anyway and see what happens. What made you want to be a writer?

Subject: Re: first question

What do you mean by writer?

Subject: writer

I guess I mean someone who writes.

Subject: Re: writer

Dear Alexa:
I've been thinking about your question. What made me want to be a writer is that I got bored and disgusted with people. That might seem counterintuitive, since writers write about people, or in any event, things having to do with people. It's the prisonhouse of language – when words are your medium, your art relies upon people for its very existence. You can't just pour paint down a mountain and call that your art. You can't make a house out of bottles and call that your art. I don't know, maybe all art is for other people, somewhere down the line, but word-art is for other people pretty much from the beginning. Unless it's word-art that takes language apart and makes it a thing or a substance. But that's not what I do. Regards, Aunt Sophie

Subject: follow-up question

Dear Aunt Sophie:
Thanks so much for answering my question. I wasn't sure what you were saying about the prisonhouse and that stuff, but my follow-up question, I guess, is why did you get bored with people?

Subject: Re: follow-up question

Why did I get bored? I don't know, but it seemed to happen very quickly. I think by the time I was eleven, I was pretty much through. How old are you? Maybe you're not old enough to have had this experience yet, but that's the age when I first started to hear people repeat themselves. It was like they were on a loop and it was all coming around again. And nobody seemed to think through what they said, they just seemed to be afraid of not having something to say, that if they stopped talking for one minute they would all fall into some great big hole. By then I'd also found out about war and murder and slavery and prison and private property and famine and the way girls are supposed to act and the way boys are supposed to act and breast implants and the Virgin Mary and seabirds getting strangled by plastic soda can rings and *the Diary of Anne Frank* and where women aren't allowed to go in a Greek Orthodox church and I thought, can't you people come up with anything better than that?

Subject: make people different

Dear Aunt Sophie:
I'm ten! So did you start writing because you wanted to make people different?

Subject: Re: make people different

I did want to make different people, Alexa, people who were more interesting than real people – or no, who were made out of the most interesting parts of real people, called characters.

Date: 11/16/03 6:57:02 PM Pacific Daylight Time

Dear Aunt Sophie: Are you coming back to Baltimore for Thanksgiving? It would be great to interview you in person. My teacher says that's really the best thing, plus I'm starting to forget what you look like.

Date: 11/16/03 11:14:03 PM Eastern Standard Time

No.

Subject: next question

Dear Aunt Sophie:
Did you move to California to become a writer?

Subject: Re: next question

I'll give you one piece of advice, Alexa, and that is this: if, for any reason, you ever feel you're doing anything less than realizing your full potential, LEAVE, leave that day, get in your car and go, don't hang around for years on end thinking things will get better, because they won't. They'll stay the same, and you'll get worse.

California's a good place to go, because it signals a definitive break. If you stop at Minnesota – or even Montana – people still think you're going to return someday, but California says you've gone as far as you possibly can without falling into the ocean. If you're that motivated to get away, you're not coming back. Our dad, your Papou, had an expression when we were growing up: "All the fruits and nuts roll to California." He put a negative spin on it, but you see what I'm getting at.

There are lots of people in California, Alexa, but there are big open spaces, too, and freeways. A "freeway" is like an "expressway" on the East Coast, only faster and more solitary. The freeways are full of people driving alone. In a better world they'd all be carpooling, but for the moment they're just trying to get away from each other. Of course, you do relate to other people on the freeway. You yield and you merge and occasionally you call the police on your cell phone to report a car with a stolen child inside. But you do all that at high speeds, so you don't form attachments.

Sometimes, when you're driving late at night, the freeway narrows down to a single lane and you see a giant yellow arrow blinking in the distance. You think when you get to it you're going to see something – something really big – but there's nothing, just the blinking arrow, and then all the lanes open up again. I like to take the freeway to the desert or the ocean –and we have both of those in California – where you can see for miles. That's the only time I feel like stopping the car and getting out.

Subject: Baltimore

Dear Aunt Sophie:
How come you wanted to get away from Baltimore so bad?

Subject: Re: Baltimore

Baltimore's not so bad, Alexa – sad, maybe, with all those empty rowhouses, but not bad, and there are sad places wherever you go. I just never got started on living there, that's all. Looking back, I think it must have been my death drive that propelled me home after college – it certainly wasn't eros. That can't have been easy on anybody, especially with a restaurant to run. Kimismeni! Papou used to bark when I was slow to take an order, or the time I was clearing away dishes and poured salad dressing all over the Mayor. Do you know any Greek, Alexa? Well in case Papou ever yells it at you, kimismeni means sleep walker. Your mom was the opposite – very quick, very on top of it.

Subject: publishing

Dear Aunt Sophie:
We don't see Papou and Yiayia as much since the restaurant closed, but whenever we do, Papou is very quiet. Mom says he's tired. Can you tell me something about your publishing experiences?

Subject: Re: publishing

Dear Alexa:
Have you ever been to Paris? When I finally got to Paris, after I'd moved to California, I sat on a bench in the Luxembourg Gardens – those are the ones with the wide paths lined with gravel that crunches under your feet and the octagonal pool where children race sailboats – and I thought, you stupid fool, you could've had a whole other life. Not that I wanted that life to be in Paris, mind you, or God forbid, among the French, but sitting there on that bench staring up at an unforgiving gray sky – the kind of sky you look into and see yourself, not cherubim or poodles or God – I was struck by how easy it would've been, if only I'd put my mind to it.

I know you don't remember what I look like, Alexa, but I remember you. In fact, the last time I saw you, I thought you showed a lot of potential. We were sitting in the living room and you were sawing away on a cello or a violin or one of the other hundreds of instruments your mother has had you playing since birth, when somebody banged through the door – your little brother maybe? Anyway, you looked up with a fierce gleam in your eye, as if to say, "Hey, I'm making music here!" and I thought, this little girl is going places, provided she doesn't fall off the trail, provided she keeps her footing as she's coming round the bend. But even if you do fall off, Alexa, you can get back on. That's what we believe out here in California.

To: 2brnt2b2@yahoo.com

That's it? No more questions?

Subject: not speaking

Dear Aunt Sophie:
I do have another question but it's not really related to my Social Studies interview and I've been wondering how to put it. How come you and my mom don't speak?

Subject: Re: not speaking

You should probably ask your mom.

Subject: Re: Re: not speaking

She says she doesn't want to talk about it.

Subject: not talking

Dear Alexa:
I can't go into it in detail, because you're only ten years old, but I just want you to know that your mom is really a kind person, underneath. She wasn't always the way she is now, so brittle and tense and humorless. When I was a kid, she was the best big sister in the world. She used to let me wear her white satin

pajamas when I was pretending to be Gino the Genie, and not many teenage girls would've done that. And when I made her a clay bowl at arts and crafts camp, she kept it right out on her bureau. "Omigod what is that, a piece of shit?" one of her friends asked, and she said, "No, it's a bowl," because she knew that I could hear them.

So your mom was a lot nicer than other big sisters and she always used to let me borrow her stuff, but the last time I pushed it too far and borrowed something I shouldn't have. I gave it back to her in good condition because that thing didn't really want to be with me, that thing only wanted to be with her in a different way, the way they were at the beginning – and honestly, that was the feeling I wanted them to recapture. It was a mistake, what I did, I know that now, but at the time my judgment was a little impaired by retsina. I just heard the exhaustion in your parents' voices that night as we were eating dinner – before you played the instrument for us in the living room and your mom put you kids to bed – and I thought to myself, somebody needs to remind these two wonderful people, who give so much to their children and their sister and their elderly parents and the business community of Baltimore, that they are living, loving creatures who deserve to have a little fun.

But like your mom said when she came back into the living room and pulled me up off the sofa by my hair, you have no right to play around in other people's lives. And I learned my lesson, Alexa, but I don't think your mom believes I learned my lesson, because she knows how bad I always was in school.

Subject: Re: not talking

Dear Aunt Sophie:
I'm surprised to hear you weren't good in school, because Mom told me you were the smartest person in our family. And the prettiest. I think so too. What did you borrow?

Date: 11/28/03 12:37:05 PM Pacific Daylight Time

Hi Aunt Sophie:
It's me Alexa again. Hope you had a Happy Thanksgiving. I don't mean to bother you, but my interview is due soon and I need to ask a few more questions. Can you tell me a little more about your publishing experiences?

Subject: experience

Dear Alexa:
Ah that our Genius were a little more of a genius! Have you ever read Emerson's essay "Experience"? I hadn't when I was ten. Life gets in the way, Alexa. That's the gist of it. You think you're taking care of things when you're buying groceries and taking vitamin C and paying credit card bills and having the brush cleared away for fire prevention, but all of that doesn't move anything forward in the other world, the world you have to make up so you can continue to live in this one. And so much of your time is taken up with recovering from the everyday shocks people deliver to you in passing – those careless little acts of uncaring, like driving a Hummer or spending fifty thousand dollars on a wedding or paying their nanny less than minimum wage. And that makes it so you have to spend more time reminding yourself of the careful little acts of caring people also perform, like offering to let you use their Vons Club card when you forget yours so you can still get the discounts, or picking up a hitchhiker in the desert even though they could get murdered by him, or not crossing a picket line. By the time you've scrawled all that out on a piece of paper, it's usually way past midnight and there's not much more you can do except take a pill and go to bed.

So to tell you the truth, Alexa, I don't have much to say about publishing, because the writing I do to make a living, technical writing, gets published automatically, and the writing I do because it keeps me alive doesn't get published at all. That about sums up my publishing experience.

Subject: favorite writers

Dear Aunt Sophie:
Wow, I didn't know you were a TECHNICAL writer! That sounds really interesting. Who are your favorite writers?

Subject: Re: favorite writers

Oh, GE. Black & Decker. Microsoft... I don't really like writers, Alexa, to tell you the truth. I mean, there's a lot of writing that I like, but the writers themselves were or are pretty miserable people. Crotchety and neurotic and self-absorbed. They call up and ask you to spend the night with them and then, just when you've finished packing your bag, call back and say they've had a breakthrough and won't be free for a while. And when you finally work up the courage to show them your own little five-page short story, they say they'll read it right away and then don't mention it again for three months until the night you finally don't agree to come over, when they say, well, based on that story you showed me, you're better off spending a little more time on your craft. No, on the whole I prefer musicians and some artists (the interventionist sort) and kindness in anyone – that's what I like. And books. I like books.

Subject: last question

Dear Aunt Sophie:
I guess this will be my last question. Do you have any advice for a young person who wants to be a writer?

Subject: Re: last question

Dear Alexa:

I've thought long and hard about your last question and this is all I have to say: be open to surprises. I know I've told you people are boring, but don't automatically assume they are, because sometimes they aren't, and those are the times you'll want to write about.

For instance, the other day I was walking near some big rocks in the desert and heard ambient music playing. I looked up and saw a rock climber and thought, oh how lame to come and play that music while you're rock climbing, what do you think this is, a fitness club? But then I said to myself – and this is where I've learned, Alexa – Sophie, don't automatically assume that guy's an idiot. So I looked more closely and saw that he'd strung a rope between two giant sandstone boulders – a simple tightrope, with no net or safety line. And right then, just as the sun was setting, he started to walk across the purple canyon formed by those two huge rocks. He wobbled in places, but he made it all the way across with that stupid music blaring, and Alexa, if that's what he needed to pull it off, blare away, because it was truly a beautiful moment, an homage to the rocks and the dying light and the empty space all around us – that great big hole everyone's afraid they'll fall into if they stop talking. And I stood there watching him with tears streaming down my face because he'd surprised me, he really had.

Of course, not all surprises are good, but even the bad ones can take you somewhere. For instance, I might never have gotten to California if I hadn't surprised your mom and dad that night. And today I just up and quit my job, because that's not the kind of writer I want to be.

So that's all the advice I have, Alexa. Oh yeah, and don't forget to write. Love, Aunt Sophie

Date: 12/5/03 6:49:01 PM Pacific Daylight Time

Dear Aunt Sophie:
I thought you would want to know we got an A on our interview!
Thank you so much, I really enjoyed doing it. I pasted in the
introduction below so you can read it.
LOVE, Alexa

My Aunt Sophie is a writer. She used to live in Baltimore, but
now she lives in California, and drives back and forth on the
freeway between the ocean and the desert. A lot of the writing
she has done is very technical, but she also writes about caring
and uncaring and surprises, and that stuff is easy to understand
if you pay attention.

One thing I learned from interviewing my Aunt Sophie is what
a character is. When my mom got really down after Aunt Sophie
moved away, my dad said, "That Sophie, what a character!" I never
knew what that meant before, but Aunt Sophie explained to me
that a character is like a person with all of the boring parts cut
out. So I guess you could say my Aunt Sophie is both a writer and
a character.

Another thing I learned from Aunt Sophie is that my mom is
really a kind person, underneath. When I showed her the interview I thought she was going to yell at me for going behind her
back, but all she did was sit with her eyes closed for a long time.
Then she opened them and looked at my dad and said maybe we
should invite Aunt Sophie back to Baltimore for Christmas.

2
JOIN HANDS

K

"Look Grace, your teacher's name is Grace, too!" Grace stops crying and turns around and looks at the name on the door, which is hers, and the beautiful black woman standing next to it, one long braid circling her head like a crown. Grace is momentarily blinded by the possibility that she might grow up to look like that, which is not in fact a possibility. When she turns around again, her mother and father are gone. It is 1973, she will learn later that day, she lives in Baltimore, Maryland, and the name of her school is Martin Luther King Junior Elementary. The other Grace steps forward and takes her hand.

This square is white. Point to something else in the classroom that is white.

1st

In kindergarten everyone played nicely together, but in first grade they're learning to read. Or not learning. Plus they don't have their own playground anymore, and at recess the other kids are bigger than they are. The violence trickles down. Grace spends most of the morning in the bathroom. Pam, a gentle girl who isn't learning to read, comes to get her. "Grace," she calls from the doorway, not even checking to see if she's in there. "Teacher says you have to come back to class." The next person who comes to get Grace is a fifth grader – Yvette, the hall monitor. Yvette kicks in the door of every stall until she kicks in the door of Grace's stall. Grace is holding a book on her lap, her pants are down. She goes back to class.

Grace is actually in love with her first grade teacher, so she doesn't really mind. Her first grade teacher is beautiful, too, but in a different way than her kindergarten teacher. She wears big silver hoop earrings and bell-bottom jeans and ties her blouse above her belly button. Sometimes she wears army pants and a canvas belt with holes in it. A giant Afro surrounds her head like a storm cloud. The older kids say she is a Black Panther. "Or a tiger," Grace says, nodding, and they call her a fool. She learns to be more careful with words.

Name the force that keeps you from floating in the air.

2nd

At lunchtime, Grace sits with the other white kids and whatever black kids don't hate them. These are usually the black kids whose parents are lawyers and journalists, or the gentle, slow ones like Pam. Most of the other white kids' parents are fixing up old row houses in the neighborhood, like Grace's parents. A few of the white kids' parents are on welfare, and those kids sit on the outer edge of the group. Altogether, the white kids and the black kids who don't hate them take up half of one long table. There are twelve long tables in the cafeteria.

One day Grace gets to school earlier than usual and stumbles upon a group of fifth grade black girls eating breakfast together in the cafeteria. At lunchtime they don't touch their free meals, they suck on blow pops instead and braid each other's hair, but at seven-thirty in the morning they line up silently, eyes crusty and hollow, and when they get their food, they sit down and eat like they need it to live. Grace backs out of the cafeteria door. She never comes to school early again.

In January, at the end of the Martin Luther King Day program, Principal Fuller tells everyone in the audience to stand up and join hands. "Go on!" he says, in his big booming voice. "Don't be shy!" Parents and teachers join hands and accompany the students through all seven verses of "We Shall Overcome," swaying rhythmically from side to side. It's weird to see her mom and dad in the middle of a school day, holding hands with black people and swaying. They've lived in the neighborhood now for three years and their house is fully remodeled, but her parents still don't have any black friends.

BICENTENNIAL HEROES

Paul Revere made a brave ride to warn the people of Boston that the _____ were coming.

3rd

In third grade Grace makes her first best friend, a girl named Nikki. Nikki is black. The fifth grade girls say she's yellow, but Nikki knows she's black. Nikki's dad runs the Afro-American newspaper, where some of the other kids' parents work, and her mom does community outreach. Her parents are divorced, and Nikki goes back and forth between their two houses.

When Grace is not at school, she thinks a lot about having a best friend. How did it happen? She had never said a single word to Nikki and then one day she did.

"Is that your drawing?"

"Yes."

"It's nice."

The next day they looked for each other in the Multipurpose Room at recess. It was raining outside.

"Hi."

"Hi."

"Do you want to play jacks?"

"Okay."

She still doesn't know how it happened.

The first time Nikki invites Grace to spend the night at her mom's house, Grace thinks her own mom may die from excitement. While Grace is packing her overnight bag, her mom stands at the window, picking Grace's model horses up off the sill and putting them back down again in the wrong order.

"Think of yourself as an ambassador," she says finally. "From our people to Nikki's people." When Grace asks her mom what an ambassador is, she says, "Somebody very, very polite."

Nikki and her mom Valerie drive up to their house the next day in a bright yellow vw bug with a loud engine. Valerie has springy black curls, like Nikki's, and she wears glamorous gold-rimmed sunglasses and a yellow halter top. Grace's mom is wearing a denim dress that ends just below her knee and a plaid hair band. She blushes and beads of sweat pop out over her upper lip. Grace has never seen her mother look so nervous. As glamorous as Valerie is, she seems nervous, too. She keeps looking around and chooses a straight back chair to sit on instead of the sofa. "Can I get you a cup of tea, Valerie?" "Thank you, Becky." Valerie smiles and relaxes a little in her chair.

For the next half an hour, Becky runs around trying to make tea for Valerie. First she can't find the tea bags and then she puts the kettle on the wrong burner, so that after twenty minutes, the water is still cold. It's a relief when Valerie finally says, "Don't worry about it, Becky. We should probably be going anyway." Grace's mom stammers an apology, but Valerie is already on the move, and Nikki and Grace follow. Grace feels a little sorry for her mom as the vw roars away, but well, she had her chance and she blew it.

The summer between third and fourth grade, Valerie takes Nikki and Grace to a barbecue down on the Chesapeake Bay. On the way there, they stop off at a church picnic so that Valerie can do outreach. Fifteen or twenty old black ladies in hats are playing bingo under a pink dogwood tree and Valerie buys Grace and Nikki their own cards, just for fun. They sit down at one of the tables while Valerie makes her rounds and Nikki shows Grace what to do. As soon as she yells BINGO, Grace knows she shouldn't have, but it's too late to take it back. When she goes up to claim her prize, nobody looks at her – not even the tiny old lady in the purple turban who checks her card and hands over the giant bottle of Jean Naté. So much for being an ambassador.

When they get to the house where the barbecue is, Nikki and Grace are the only kids. There's music playing and the grownups are all dancing. Grace asks if it's a wedding. It is not. The two girls change into their swimsuits and clamber down the sandy bank to the beach. The bay is still, like the air, and there are flies everywhere. Nikki drops her towel on the sand and runs in. Grace tests the water first with her toes. It's warm, like the air. She tells Nikki that she's never been in the bay before, only the ocean.

"Black people didn't used to be allowed in the ocean."

"Oh."

Nikki knows a lot about where black people didn't used to be allowed, because her dad is always reminding her. Nikki's dad hates the bay because of the flies and because there are jellyfish. Whenever Nikki stays with him, they go to the ocean.

"I like the bay, though, it's like taking a bath."

Grace agrees. "It's nice."

She gets in and floats on her back for a while like Nikki, enjoying the bay. Then she gets scared of jellyfish and stands up.

Nikki stands up too and stretches out her hands. Grace takes hold and they jump up and place the soles of their feet together, pushing hard until their butts collide and they both flip over. Next time Grace stretches out her hands and Nikki takes hold. They go back and forth, round and round like that, churning the soft warm water with their bodies until Valerie calls down time to eat.

Why are communities alike in some ways and different in others?

Why are communities located in the places they are?

Does the community shape nature as much as nature shapes the community?

What causes communities to change?

4th

There's a new fourth grade teacher, Miss Myers, who is white. Everybody hates her, especially the white kids. She's a disgrace. She has no authority and no one listens to a word she says. Her students hang out of the windows all day long and yell at passers-by. Grace has never been in such an out-of-control classroom. At first Miss Myers tells them to behave, then she asks them to behave, then she begs. Finally she falls silent and stares into her coffee cup like she's at home at her kitchen table and they aren't even there. Is she humming?

But one day Miss Myers strikes back, starting in on a black kid named Darvon as she's calling out the roll. Everything about Miss Myers is different that day. Her hair is in a bun and she's put on some kind of business suit instead of the long hippy skirts she usually wears.

"Darvon? I want to tell you something." Miss Myers smiles and the kids at the window take their seats, sensing she's about to be cruel. Finally. "Did you know that Darvon's the name of a painkiller? They probably gave it to your mother when she was in labor." Miss Myers is laughing so hard now she can barely speak. "Did you know your mother named you after a goddamn painkiller?"

The question hangs in the air, the room is eerily quiet. The class is staring at Miss Myers, open-mouthed, and Darvon is covering his ears.

In January they have to watch the TV miniseries Alex Haley's *Roots* at home and write a report on it for Social Studies. Terrance Matthews pushes Grace into the lockers the morning after Part One.

"Your great-granddaddy whipped my great-granddaddy!"

"No, no!" Grace says, once she's regained her balance. "My great-granddaddy lived in Russia!" She isn't normally so quick with a comeback, but she'd prepared her response on the way to school. "And my other great-granddaddy was in Nova Scotia!"

Terrance shrugs and shoves her into the lockers again.

Slavery was a terrible thing, Grace begins her Social Studies report. She doesn't know how to go on.

In the spring, Nikki tells her they can't be best friends anymore. They can't even talk to each other anymore.

"Why not?"

"Because you're a whitegirl and my daddy says you'll only hurt me some day."

Grace has no comeback for this. Silently, she stretches out her hands, but Nikki backs away from her and out of the classroom. Her new best friend, a black girl named Tasha, is waiting in the hall.

Grace makes it through the rest of the day by looking out the window at a dogwood tree and humming to herself, like Mrs. Myers. That night at the dinner table she tells her parents.

"He's just trying to protect his daughter," Grace's own dad says with a sigh. "I can understand that."

Grace's fork clangs onto her plate. "But what about what Dr. King said? What about the day when little black boys and black girls will be able to join hands with little white boys and white girls as sisters and brothers?"

Her dad turns up his palms. "I guess that day isn't here yet, honey."

Her mom makes a weird noise and covers her mouth with a napkin.

Abraham Lincoln, Rosa Parks and Martin Luther King all stood up for their beliefs. Tell about how these people made a difference in the world next to their pictures. On a separate sheet of paper, tell how YOU can make a difference.

5th

Grace knows better than to try to talk to Nikki ever again. That's why she's surprised and panicked to find herself standing in front of her on the first day of school, blocking her way. How did she get there? Nikki looks a little panicked, too, but Tasha knows exactly what to do. She takes Nikki's elbow and keeps walking and talking, moving through Grace like a mist.

Grace visits the private school she will attend the following year. There are no black girls there. There are no boys either. At dinner, her parents explain that this is the school Grace must go to in order to get into college. Many of her classmates at Martin Luther King Junior Elementary will not go to college, they say. Grace has never thought about this before, but she sees instantly that it's true.

Her parents have begun to look at other houses, in other parts of town.

"How much do you think you can get for your place, now that it's all fixed up?" their family friends ask.

"We never expected to make a profit," her father says.

"It wasn't about that for us," her mother says, and their friends nod respectfully.

Grace decides to forget about the new school and the new house until she absolutely has to remember. There's something more pressing she needs to deal with. Nikki and Tasha are going to sing a Peaches & Herb duet, "Reunited," in the school talent show. She's seen them practicing in Mrs. Bristow's classroom. Mrs. Bristow is the music teacher and the talent show director, and she's coaching them after school. They sound fantastic. They look amazing. Grace is so jealous she thinks it may kill her. Literally poison her – she can feel acid collecting at the back of her throat.

She casts about for someone, anyone, she can enter the Talent Show with, and turns up a white girl with long red hair named Skye. She barely knows Skye, who only came to their school in the fourth grade, but she chooses her because her mom is a hippy and hippies are creative people. Too creative, maybe. Skye's mom tells the girls to pick a song off her Yoko Ono album if they really want to blow people's minds. While Grace and Skye are listening to the record, which sounds really weird, Skye's mom tells them the story of how Yoko Ono met John Lennon. John was goofing around with the other Beatles at one of Yoko's art shows, making fun of everything, when Yoko came over and told him to go up a flight of stairs and open the little door in the wall at the top. John went up the stairs and opened the little door. "Inside," says Skye's mother, her eyes wide and bright, "was the word YES."

The song Grace and Skye end up choosing is "Touch Me," and Skye choreographs a complicated dance to it that involves a lot of mime. It's hard to tell what the tune is when Yoko's singing, though, or even to keep time, and when they audition Mrs. Bristow tells them they just don't have it together. Grace blames Skye for the stupid dance (which isn't really fair) and Skye blames Grace for not being able to carry a tune (which isn't fair either) and Mrs. Bristow tells them to take it outside. So much for YES. The talent show goes on without them and Nikki and Tasha come in second, losing out to a girl who will one day star in a television movie about the Supremes. Even Grace must concede that Nikki and Tasha really do have it together. Even Grace wishes they had won.

Songs have power through their words and/or melody. Tell about a song that has a message or particular meaning in your life.

Graduation

The very last time Grace sings "We Shall Overcome" in public is at her fifth grade graduation. From up onstage, she sees her parents join hands with their black neighbors for the last time, too. They look a little sheepish, but they do it. Everyone joins hands, even the kids crowded onto the stage – the entire graduating class. Nikki is up there somewhere, but Grace doesn't look for her. That's all behind her now. She's looking into the audience, into the future. Mrs. Bristow starts up the piano with a grand arpeggio.

"'We Shall Overcome!'" Principal Fuller booms. "Sing it like you mean it!"

And they do.

3
WARMING THE WORLD

Kerista was a group marriage commune active in San Francisco from 1971–1991. Upon joining the commune, all members agreed to uphold the group's 84 Social Standards, and assumed new, three-letter names that were acronyms for important ideas or values. In the late eighties, Kerista founded Abacus, a highly successful Bay Area computer business and the first Apple dealership to be woman-owned and operated.

While this story quotes extensively from the Kerista's 84 Social Standards, all characters and events are fictional.

THURSDAY

Growth Group has been getting a little too intense lately, everybody agrees. It was Jed's idea to keep this journal instead, get it all out in writing, say how we really feel. Of course, Jed's the one who's been hard-vibing the whole house, but okay. We all agree not to discuss group dynamics outside of here, though, right? I think that's the only way it can really work. And since today was supposed to be my turn in Growth Group, I'm going first.

How do I feel? Tired. Kept waking up last night. The fact is, I don't sleep well with anyone but Von. Tonight the Sleep Rotation has me paired with Dan, who likes to cuddle all night long in a pool of sweat, and tomorrow is Jed, who prides himself on making it no less than three times per "session," as he calls it (sigh)! Saturday it's Sal, who's a restless sleeper, and I have to wait until Sunday to be with Von. He's the only one who seems to understand where I'm at. We get into bed as soon as dinner's over and sleep until breakfast. No sex. Sometimes we even forget to take

off our shoes. It's gotten so that whenever I even see him, a wave of exhaustion hits and I have to look the other way.
–Ava

I've noticed Ava's been feeling pretty sex-negative these days. The dyadic lovejoy I experienced last night with BEA, on the other hand, was out of this world! FOUR times, Ava! FOUR TIMES!
–Jed

Like I care?
–Ava

I recommend Ava review Social Standard #23 – Sense of Humor/ Non-Touchiness/ Absence of Grimness.
–Jed

I recommend Jed not recommend things for me to do.
–Ava

Wow! I mean, bad wow! Jed and Ava are both such beautiful people, it hurts my heart to read this. Maybe Ava just needs some time off from the Sleeping Rotation. Or maybe she should be allowed to sleep with Von more than once a week. She looks so down these days, and when she first came to the house she was so happy and full of life.
–Bea

I wouldn't mind sleeping with Ava more than once a week.
–Von

FRIDAY
EXCUSE ME? The whole point of this commune, or have you all forgotten, is POLYfidelity! Aren't we trying something new here? More sex, and also more love? An end to jealousy and emotional boredom? An end to loneliness? Deep, meaningful relation-ships with MORE THAN ONE PERSON? A responsible HEDONISM? Genuine COMMUNITY? I remind you, we all committed to each

other EQUALLY when we signed on. Plus we all committed to the 84 Social Standards, to keep us from falling back into old, dead-end patterns. In other words, we SIGNED a CONTRACT. Christ, I was the one who brought Ava to the house in the first place! No, I don't think Ava and Von should sleep together more than once a week! This is a FAMILY, goddamnit!
–Jed

Cool out, man.
–Von

Would you like to say a little more, Von? Need I remind you of Social Standard #5 – Verbality? To refresh your memory: "Conversation is an art form everyone can develop (and should). Nonverbality is unsocial, and antithetical to personal mental health development and friendship formation."
–Jed

Nope, that's all I have to say, Jed. Oh, wait a minute. You win.
–Von

Von? Social Standard #36 – Assertiveness. "Clearly speaking one's mind and expressing one's true feelings on any given Subject is a positive value, regardless of what any other individuals may think."
–Jed

hey krazy kats krazy kats krazykatskrazykats
with my third i eye see the truth
loneliness makes men krazy its
time for a ball a beautiful ball beautiful
balling a beautiful ball
–sal

I don't think family members should write in the commune journal while they're tripping. Agreed? Sal's individual quest for enlightenment is preventing him from fully participating in our group experiment.
–Jed

Dear Family:
My first entry in the group journal. Gotta get used to writing instead of talking. Weird. What are you thinking as you read this? It's so impersonal. By the way, it's me, Dan, the man who likes to cuddle (argh)! I can't help it, it's true! I appreciate the ladies so much for all they do, but the two nights a week I have to sleep alone are pretty hard to get through, too.
–Dan

SATURDAY
Wow. I mean, good wow. The house is so quiet this morning, I can hear it breathing. You breathing. My family. Got up early and left Sal asleep in bed, his shiny black hair spread out all over. Beautiful. He didn't come down from his trip until around four am, and then he crashed. He said he really got through to the other side this time, and I believe him.

I was too excited to sleep after he came in, though, because I kept thinking about tonight. It's the commune birthday party – we're one year old! I got up at six to bake the cake and it's cooling here in front of me on the kitchen table. I was thinking about the giant log that made this tabletop, how old the tree must've been when they cut it down. I wonder if we'll be – the commune will be – around as long as this beautiful tree was. I hope so.
–Bea

Has it really been a year? Feels like five years. Just kidding. I do want this thing to work. I love you guys – and girl.
–Ava

Okay, has anyone seen my hammer? I need to put up the stage for the party tonight.

–Von

Von? It's a communal hammer, isn't it?

–Jed

Has anyone seen our hammer? We need to put up the stage for the band tonight.

–Von

Sorry man, I don't have time to help out, but I remember about the hammer now. I loaned it to the people who just moved in across the street, some really cool cats.

–Jed

I see. Well, maybe you could ask the really cool cats to bring it back.

–Von

I'll see what I can do, man. In the meantime, check out Social Standard #68 – No Uptightness.

–Jed

Dear Family:

It's me again, Dan. Do I have to identify myself each time or do you recognize my handwriting? Weird. Anyway, I met a fine young lady down in the Panhandle today, wearing a buckskin dress. Her name is Maya and I think she may be the answer to all of our problems, or some of them anyway. She's very interested in the commune and may want to join! I was thinking Ava might not feel so overwhelmed if there were more female vibrations in the house – not just hers and Bea's – and another woman in the Rotation would mean the men would only have to sleep alone one night instead of two. Anyway, I'm bringing Maya to the party tonight so you can meet her. I sense the potential for a beautiful connection. See what you think!

–Dan

Okay, but like the Standards say, No Acceptance of Anything on
Blind Faith.
–Jed

SUNDAY
dancing freaks you beautiful
free love freeks
touched the
buckskin lady's swaying black hair
her hair? my hair?
it parts   like a curtain
on the other side we're all won
–sal

So it looks like Sal had a good time last night. How about everyone
else? What did you think of Maya? We stayed up talking until the
sun came up, she said you were some crazy beautiful people and
she was seriously digging the whole scene.
–Dan

Last night was like old times, wasn't it? Wow! All of those funky
people – where did they come from? And that wayout band, with
the fuzzy white helmets. A beautiful celebration of a beautiful
idea! And Maya's gorgeous, too. What a lovely name! What does
it mean?
–Bea

I talked to Maya for hours last night, she's fantastic! So warm and
uninhibited. Then I danced until morning and today I'm not even
tired. I would love to have her in the house. Such good vibes. I feel
happy, like everything's starting over.
–Ava

Seems like a pretty cool lady to me.
–Von

I only saw Maya from across the room – man, that was some crowd, practically all of Lower Haight was there – but I say we work her into the Rotation right away. Then we can have a Growth Group meeting to process everything, and THEN we can decide on letting her into the Family.

–Jed

Right on, and since this is one of my solo nights, I say start the new Rotation with me! Maya's packing her stuff to come over right now.

–Dan

MONDAY
Dear Family:
I found out what "Maya" means last night. The power of a god or goddess to make a concept into reality. Amen.

–Dan

TUESDAY
ogodogodogoddess

–sal

WEDNESDAY
That is one hot mama.

–Von

THURSDAY
So... Maya didn't feel like getting it on last night. She says she still has to get used to the idea of being with a cat her dad's age – groovy, long-lasting and massively experienced though he may be. She admits she's still got some Family of Origin Neuroses, but she says she's going to work on them. Of course, I was a little disappointed, especially after reading all of your entries, but I confirmed with her that the Sleeping Rotation is NOT a "sex schedule." To tell you the truth, it was good practice in Non-Salaciousness – Social Standard #73. Check it out fellas!

–Jed

FRIDAY

So much for Maya. Too bad. Everyone agrees she's out after Growth Group, right? I mean, she's sexy alright, but what a nutjob! Textbook Willful Non-Cooperation!
–Jed

No way. I thought she was great. I want her. In. I want her in.
–Dan

Are you crazy? What about all of her Irrational, Emotionally Unqualified Intonations?
–Jed

I thought Maya was extremely rational. In fact, I thought she made the most sense I've heard around here in a long time. And I appreciated her Willingness to Ask Questions.
–Von

What about what she said to Bea? That was downright Willful Malevolence!
–Jed

Not at all. I appreciated what Maya had to say to me. I mean, sure, I was a little taken aback by some of her comments – especially when she told me I might have big tits but that didn't mean I had to be the house wet nurse. But then I remembered what the Standards say: No One Can Insult Me Without My Own Consent, plus Colorful, Earthy Language is Okay. She was right, and I accept Responsibility for the Consequences of My Speech and Actions. The kitchen is a big mess, and this time I'm not going to clean it up.
–Bea

I thought Maya asked some really good questions, such as how we can all live by a social contract that was drawn up by only one member of our group, "groovy, long-lasting and massively experienced" though he may be (!) She's right: it contradicts the

Standards of Equality and Participatory Democracy.
–Ava

Yeah, and I liked what she had to say about how rule-bound we all seemed. How we're really groovy and really uptight at the same time. I think we're so afraid of repeating our parents' mistakes that we cling to this set of Standards and try to conform every situation to them. As a result we never grow.
–Dan

heavy
–sal

Can I help it if I was the first one to have the DREAM of polyfidelity and the GUTS to put it into practice? It's not my fault I was a generation ahead of my time. Dan, Ava, you read the Standards before you signed on. Nobody made you do it.
–Jed

I know I did, Jed, and I thought it was fantastic at the time – truly visionary. But things change. Speaking of which, Maya had another great idea today. She's been working at Berkeley Computers, and she thinks if she can get access to their mainframe after hours, it may be possible to put the Sleep Rotation on a spreadsheet. Then you could see your whole month – or even year – of partners at a glance! She says advanced forms of being require advanced forms of technology.
–Dan

NO! I still say no.
–Jed

Jed? Social Standard #77 – Non-Stodginess in the Face of Overwhelming Evidence. "When a vote or opinion poll goes unanimously against the way one person is voting, she/he is expected to go along with the vote cheerfully, giving the weight of the group mind perspective due respect."

I think she's in, man.
–Von

Friday

Okay, so it's back to the journal again. Well I am NOT going to apologize for my behavior in Growth Group these past few weeks. Do you expect me to just stand by and watch my dream unravel? CAN'T YOU SEE WHAT'S HAPPENING??!! Ava and Von are in dyadic withdrawal from the group – as, I might add, are MAYA and BEA!! Not that I have a problem with ladies loving ladies – on the contrary – but where does that leave me, Dan and Sal? More importantly, where does it leave the COMMUNE? To call this a Sleep Rotation at all is a joke. It's just plain old monogamy plus some singles. Plain old boring, exclusive, backwards, conformist, exploitative monogamy!
–Jed

I'm not too happy about the situation either, but Maya says Lady's Choice is long overdue and I think she's probably right. I say we go along with it and maybe we'll get a turn again soon.
–Dan

MAYBE we'll get a TURN? This is why we need the STANDARDS!
–Jed

Hey cats, how about we drop the whole Sleep Rotation thing and concentrate on stuff that really matters, like opposing this goddamn evil war? And what's happening right here to the Bay, all of that illegal dumping – did you see the article Maya's been circulating? She's right, we could do a lot of good in the world, given Kerista's long history of communication and cooperation.
–Von

Easy for YOU to say, Von, you're getting LAID. Right?
–Jed

You better believe it.
–Ava

SATURDAY
Wow! I just want to share with you all that this is the best thing that's ever happened to me. Being with Maya, I mean – exclusively. I've achieved a level of joy with her I now want everywhere else in my life, and it makes me want to change the world. End war, like Von said. Stop pain. A love like this demands love of the planet. I mean, that's what we're really after, isn't it? That's what the Standards were guiding us towards, right?
–Bea

Never having had the JOY OF MAYA, I wouldn't know.
–Jed

SUNDAY
Oh, Jed. It's so much bigger than that. So much bigger. But now Maya thinks maybe we should cut out all sex in the house for the time being. Then nobody will feel left out and everyone can channel their energies into making posters and stuff. And maybe we could clean up the house so it doesn't look so much like a fleabag motel and you know, really center ourselves.
– Bea

Von & I are willing to try it, for the sake of the Family.
–Ava

EXCUSE ME for pointing this out, but isn't there a NAME for a celibate commune that does good works? Like MONASTARY?
–Jed

MONDAY
HELLO? No one talks to me around the house anymore and now no one responds to my JOURNAL entries??!!
–Jed

TUESDAY

FAMILY? Need I remind you? Social Standard #69 – No Psychological Withdrawal. "No withdrawing into a shell in which issues and feelings are stored in the head which should be aired and talked out. There should be an active willingness at all times to raise problems and unclear issues for group mind consideration, and no avoidance of this process."
–Jed

WEDNESDAY

Jed, I know you're feeling left out and unappreciated and confused by all of the changes in the house, and I just want to say, I'll never forget the day I met you. You were sitting on the curb outside the Krishna bakery on Haight with the sunlight playing in that long red beard of yours and I swear, when you looked at me I felt like you could see into my soul. And all of the things you had to say about human possibility were so amazing: how we'd been raised to compete and not cooperate, hate and not love, obey and not resist, but how deep down inside of each of us there was this hard little kernel of freedom, and if we watered it, it would grow. And then you told me your given name was Cecil but you'd renamed yourself Justice Equals Democracy, or Jed for short. And I said my name was Melanie and you said, how about Beauty Elicits Actualization? Remember that? When you gave me my new name?
–Bea

REMEMBER? Is it all OVER then? Don't you miss me just a LITTLE, Bea?
–Jed

Miss you? I see you all the time!
–Bea

But not THAT way. Remember how good it was? We always had a special connection, the two of us. CHEMISTRY. Remember?
–Jed

Maya says stop with the hard vibe if you know what's good for you.
–Bea

Oh? And what's MAYA's trip? Maybe she should respond herself once in a while, instead of always speaking through you. Is she afraid to leave a PAPER TRAIL?
–Jed

THURSDAY
Okay everyone, time out. Sal's been drafted. What are we going to do?
–Ava

Sal's been DRAFTED? But Sal's INSANE!
–Jed

As if that matters to Uncle Sam. No question – Sal has to make a run for it. Wish I had.
–Von

Maya knows a way into British Columbia. She and I could drive Sal up this weekend.
–Bea

We want to come, too.
–Ava + Von

Don't forget me!
–Dan

FRIDAY
Okay, so lets make it a Family trip then! Maya has a cabin in B.C. she inherited from her old man. Plenty of land, too. Maybe we should stay for a while?
–Bea

At least long enough to scope out the draft dodging community.
Like Maya says, we could help out a lot more guys in Sal's situation. She thinks we could adapt the search and retrieval system
she's been working on at Berkeley Computers to keep track of all
the routes into Canada plus contact names and temporary housing.
And to think the Draft Board's still using ping pong balls!
—Ava

Groovy! I was thinking though, maybe we should stay even longer
than that... the possibilities are just so... great.
—Bea

I see what you mean. Are you thinking what I'm thinking? Maybe
it's time to start another... experiment in living?
—Ava

We've never tried the rural thing. I think it's safe to say we've got
urban communal living down — sharing public assistance, alter-
nating temporary employment — but Von's the only one here who
really knows how to use his hands.
—Bea

I'll say.
—Ava

I've been wanting to get back to the land.
—Von

I'd be into it, too. I'm not much of a carpenter, but I'm willing to
learn. And I used to be a beekeeper.
—Dan

A beekeeper? Really? Where?
—Ava

When I was a kid in Nebraska.
—Dan

You're from Nebraska? I can't believe I didn't know that. How did you end up in San Francisco?
—Ava

Same as the rest of us, I guess. Jed came through my town on a hog with that long red beard flapping over his shoulder. I swear from far away it looked like he was on fire. I was working at the gas station, and I filled up his tank. We had a twenty-minute conversation and a week later I was on my way to S.F.
—Dan

Same here. I met Jed outside the bus station in L.A., on my way back from Saigon. Or maybe he met me. Nobody else showed up, that's for sure. He bought me a cup of coffee and we talked for maybe half an hour, and at the end of that half hour he offered me a ride up North.
—Von

Okay, so say we were to do this thing in Canada. Would there have to be another Sleep Rotation?
—Bea

Dear Family: I know you're all expecting me to say yes because I hate to sleep alone, but the truth is... I've met someone. She wants to move to the country and she knows how to make yogurt, too! What I'm saying is—all of a sudden I'm not so interested in sharing! Not on that level... weird... never thought this could happen to me...
—Dan

SATURDAY
YOGURT? No SHIT! You people are PATHETIC. I just found the journal behind the refrigerator and I am NOT AMUSED by your SECRET CONVERSATION. You think that's all there is to founding a COMMUNE??!! WOODWORKING AND BEEKEEPING AND YOGURT?! What has Maya DONE to you? Are you just going to follow her WHEREVER? Pair off & trot onto her ark like dumb little ANIMALS??!!

I DEMAND to speak to Maya. And you, FAMILY, better think long and hard about why SHE'S SITTING OUT THIS CONVERSATION!
–Jed

SUNDAY
jed, please stop shouting.
–maya

????
–Jed

all of those aggressive caps.
–maya

is this better?
–jed

it's a start.
–maya

can we speak in private, maya? one on one? if the answer's yes, leave the journal on top of the fuse box.
–jed

MONDAY
– what did you want to say to me, jed?
– are you really taking my commune to Canada?
– i'm not taking "your" commune anywhere. any other questions?
– why wouldn't you ever make love to me?
– because you made such an issue of it.
– okay.
– okay?
– okay i get it. i do believe in that kernel of freedom, you know, like Bea said.
– really?
– really.
– because i'm not unattracted to you, jed.

– we share a lot of the same values, don't we?
– to tell the truth, i've never met anyone i connected with on so many things.
– but you were afraid to show it? afraid i'd manipulate our connection? is that why you stayed away from me? because you were scared, maya?
– maybe. yes.
– don't be.

THURSDAY

Maya! I can't believe what I'm reading here! And I can't believe you hid the journal from the rest of us! What about Canada? What about our fresh start in the country?
–Dan

I'm starting to think it would be wrong to give up on what you started here with Jed. The basic structure and principles are sound – these could just be growing pains.
–Maya

Maya? Baby? Are you getting it on with that fuckhead?
–Bea

Bea! Need I remind you of ss #83 – No Profanity? "The use of words such as 'fuck' or 'shit' is not considered profane so long as they are used in a literal context (that is, to describe the act of sexual intercourse or the excretory function). Using the same words, however, as derogatory epithets or in other imprecise ways is believed to muddy up communication and lower the aesthetic standard of conversation."
–Maya

How can you take a situation like this and slap a number on it? I love you.
–Bea

I love you too, Bea, and so does Jed. And everyone else in the house.
–Maya

I don't want to be loved by everybody. I want to be loved by you.
–Bea

Oh honey. This is why we have the Standards. It's too hard otherwise.
–Maya

You are fucking him, aren't you?
–Bea

Bea, we don't need Maya and Jed to start our commune in the country. Them or their bullshit contract.
–Ava + Von

I know. I know. I just–wow. I don't know about starting all over again, without Maya and without any Standards at all... I feel lost. Am I lost? Are we lost? There's still something beautiful here, isn't there?
–Bea

Yes, and what's beautiful can't be made into a contract. It can't even be put into words.
–Ava + Von

Correction–or no, excuse me, suggestion: what's beautiful must be put into words, or it will disappear.
–Jed

I think Jed has a point.
–Maya

Argh! We're right back where we started!
–Dan

beautiful freeks
i understand you
need to work some things
out but my ball is up

had a vision last night a
cold dark ball the earth
abandoned by the universe
      but then
      there you were
      all of you
      naked on a giant bed of light
      & the light   red light
                        was moving out all over

i was looking down from
outer space or maybe
canada & you were trying to
make it better you were
warming the world

–sal

4
ALIEN ENCOUNTER

When people asked her if she was still looking for that "special someone," she said no. I've tried them all, men and women – or at least enough to draw conclusions – and though they certainly have strong qualities, I think I've reached the limits of human connection. What a pity, people said, as if they didn't believe her. Such terrible disappointment in one so young. I'm telling you, she told them, our relationships are programmed to self-destruct. All that remains to be seen is if you're going to puddle together or flail apart, and that you can usually tell within five minutes of meeting a person. Oh, I'm in a bad way, all right, the way you are when there are no more surprises.

She didn't tell them that for some time now she'd been looking for that *extra*-special someone. She didn't think it was any of their business. Not the people in L.A. Her neighbors in the desert were another matter. They understood that it was her last hope, encountering an alien, and that was why she'd left L.A. for a windswept plain above the town of Yucca Valley. It had been their last hope, too.

"It'll happen," they said. "Just be patient."

They rehearsed the signs of an alien encounter with her, so that she would be prepared: missing time, feeling paralyzed when you're lying in bed, waking up in a different place than where you went to sleep, being prone to addictive behaviors, having sexual or relationship problems, feeling drawn to remote areas. Having the urge to build a fence around your property out of cereal boxes might be considered one, too, although it wasn't in the literature. The number one sign that you'd had an alien encounter was when you exhibited such behaviors but couldn't remember having had an alien encounter.

All of her neighbors had shown one or more of the symptoms in the short time she'd known them, so she thought her own chances of running into an alien in her neck of the woods were pretty good. Her nearest neighbor, Mike, a highway maintenance worker, hadn't gotten out of bed since his encounter on a lonely road up north near Baker.

"Mike," she whispered, when no one else was around. "Do you feel paralyzed?"

"Paralyzed," Mike murmured, rolling over to face the wall.

Meanwhile, the woman who owned the house next to Mike's kept waking up outside on her picnic table, and the guy in the next house over, the one with the cereal box fence, was seriously addicted to painkillers. So there was obviously plenty of paranormal activity going on in her area. Plus her house was just south of Giant Rock, where the Alien Contact Society is headquartered, not to mention the name of her road was Jupiter Avenue.

"The perfect location for your home buying needs," her anorexic Yucca Valley realtor confirmed. Closing in on the sale, she confessed she herself had experienced a false pregnancy after sharing her bed with an alien.

"Don't know if I'll ever get my figure back," she said, inspecting her stomach, which was flat as a board.

The Sheriff had a story, too – he'd been chasing down a speeding motorist when a towering blue flame appeared to the left of the highway, way out on Indian land. Naturally, he abandoned pursuit of the speeder and headed up the hill towards the flash. When he came over the top, he saw a little egg-shaped vehicle parked in the valley below.

"At first I thought it was one of those electric cars," he said. "But when I saw two little kids get out, and no adults, I got suspicious. Plus they were wearing white coveralls, which is not something children normally wear around here. So I radioed my partner and told him I need backup. He says it's probably just a couple of NASCAR mechanics out on a test drive, and I say what mechanic you know wears white coveralls? Painters, then, he says, they're probably painters, and I say, what the hell is there to paint out here?"

Despite the obvious force of the Sheriff's argument, his partner took his time getting there, and as a result, the Sheriff was the only one to witness the orange ball of light that burned the back of his neck as the alien spacecraft took off. Oh, his partner witnessed the burn, but not the ball, and that, more than anything, seemed to be what really bothered the Sheriff – the way his buddy let him down.

Her own encounter, when it finally did take place, occurred at dusk in early March, as she was walking along the dirt road that went from her property to nowhere and to more nowhere beyond that. The wind had died down and the sky was turning pink and gold when she spotted the alien at the place where a spiky green Joshua tree split the road in two.

He was leaning against the tree, looking out at the horizon. Rather than white coveralls, he wore a silver windbreaker and a purple ski cap that accentuated the enormous size of his head, the way caps do on babies. He was the height of a very short man, not quite a "little person," and his eyes, which were huge and black, were also heavy-lidded. Bedroom eyes, she thought suddenly, and wondered if the alien had telepathically projected the idea into her head. His hands were like shells, with no fingers. She wondered what they could do. He was wearing dusty black running shoes, so she couldn't see his feet.

She walked right up and said hello. She'd waited a very long time for this moment, and wasn't about to let it slip away. The alien turned his enormous head and lifted his chin in her direction.

"'Sup," he said, in a voice like a snake rattle, playing it cool.

"Are you lost?" she asked politely.

The alien's gray face turned the color of his ski cap. He laughed, a little heh-heh like a cat bringing up a hairball, and kicked at the ground.

"Well," he said, rubbing his little alien nostrils. "The sign said Jupiter."

"Ah," she said, charmed, and resisted the impulse to wrap her arms around him. She wasn't sure yet if he had any bones.

"Are you hungry?" she asked.

The alien nodded, tears springing to his eyes. "Terribly hungry."

"What do you eat?"

"Cheese," he said, and smiled. She caught a glimpse of black gums, no teeth.

That was lucky, because she didn't cook. If the alien had said he ate beef stroganoff, their encounter might have ended right there and then. As it was, the two of them walked back down the road to her house to get some cheese, chatting about this and that. Almost as a formality, he asked her to take him to her leader, but she said her leader was very far away, in Washington, and it probably wasn't a good idea to go see him anyway.

"Now isn't a great time to be an alien in America," she said. "They're really cracking down on illegal immigration."

She asked if the alien's spaceship had left without him and he said it was okay, he'd only been hitching a ride.

"I'm not one of those aliens on a mission," he said. "I just wanted to get out and see the universe."

She nodded. Wanderlust was something she understood.

"I didn't think it would be so hard to get off of Earth again, though," he said. "I didn't realize your shuttles were for government use only."

"Have you ever been in a house?" she asked, as they turned into her property.

"Once," he said. "There was this nice lady down in Yucca Valley who–"

"Was she a realtor?" she asked sharply, with a pang of jealousy. "Really skinny?"

"Realtor?" The alien looked confused.

"Let's see about that cheese," she said, softening, and the alien nodded, licking his thin blue lips.

It turned out the alien didn't need fingers because he could do all kinds of things to the cheese just by waving his hands over it. Fast slicing and fine juliennes. When he waved his hands towards his mouth, the cheese floated into it.

"Electromagnetic fields," he said when he caught her watching him, and winked. A charge ran through her, from her fingers to her toes.

They took the cheese out into the yard and lay wrapped in blankets on purple lawn chairs looking up at the night sky. She thought the alien would be able to tell her all about the stars, but the only constellations he could spot were the Dippers. She had to show him Orion.

"Is one of those stars your planet?" she asked dreamily.

The alien shrugged. "I guess so. Everything looks different from here."

She looked over at the alien and he held her gaze for a long time. Not in a hypnotizing or brainwashing way, it was more a look of recognition, as if he knew what she wanted and thought she should have it. What did she want, now that she'd encountered her alien? She wasn't sure.

"Can you read my mind?" she asked.

"I don't know," said the alien.

She put the alien to bed on an air mattress in her living room. She thought he would be impressed by the technology–how the mattress pumped itself up and everything–but he didn't seem all that interested. She was starting to get the feeling the alien wasn't very good at science, which must've been hard for him back on his planet, because most aliens are.

But he definitely had something, a certain charisma, a way with people–or with her, anyway. All night long, from the moment her head hit the pillow in the other room, she had nonstop sex dreams about him. In her dreams, he was waving his shell-hands over her and causing clitorises and vaginas to form all over her body. He himself had two sex organs, a cute little blue one shaped like a dolphin and a big veiny purple one, which was kind of alarming-looking. With all of that equipment in play, there was seemingly no end to the positions in which she could receive pleasure and give pleasure in return. When she awoke the next morning she was utterly exhausted.

She stumbled into the living room expecting to find it had all been a dream, but there was the alien standing by the window, wearing the orange silk robe she'd lent him over his windbreaker. With that big bald head, he looked like a Buddhist monk, and she was overcome by shame. Here, in her home, was a visitor from another planet – practically a holy man – and all she could think about was s-e-x?

She spelled the word out in her head, because she still wasn't sure if he could read her mind. Although if he could, she suddenly realized, then he could also spell.

"Good morning," the alien said, with a little bow. "How can I ever repay you for the kindness you have shown me?"

"How about some weeding?" she blurted out before he read her mind any further. "We had a record rainfall last winter and my yard is totally overgrown."

The alien bowed again and went outside to weed her yard in the fiery dawn. She stood at the window watching him pass his hands over the plants and wave them out of the ground. He was better than a hula hoe, because he pulled them out by the roots. After he'd done that job, she asked him to patch the roof on her shed, and when that took him less than five minutes, to repair and paint her entire house.

They went down to the hardware store in Yucca Valley to get supplies. To her surprise, nobody batted an eye when the alien walked in. Then she looked around at all the leathery old desert denizens browsing for stop valves and duct tape and rubber tubing. Mystery solved.

Her house was falling down and it turned out to be a big job to repair and sand and paint it, even for an alien with electromagnetic fields at his disposal. It took three whole days – the happiest three days of her life. Every day, after the alien knocked off work, they would eat cheese and look up at the stars or listen to country music and talk about their childhoods. She'd grown up in a large, close-knit family who all thought she was crazy for wanting to live in the desert. No matter how many photos she showed them of bobcats and scorpions and diamondback rattlers, they still thought she was crazy.

On the second day, she told the alien about a dream she'd had the night before. In her dream, her entire extended family – parents, grandparents, aunts, uncles, brothers and cousins – was in the living room waiting to meet the alien, who was in the bathroom, and they kept saying, "Why can't we see him? We want to see him," and she kept saying, "He's in the bathroom, leave him alone. Give him some privacy."

The alien nodded and said, "Of course, that's you in the dream, you are the alien in the bathroom," and she thought that was very wise. Then the alien talked about the creatures he'd grown up with, not exactly a family – it sounded more like a lab. In any event, they were really straight-laced, and never laughed or played music or lay wrapped in blankets on purple lawn chairs eating cheese. Around them, the alien had always felt like he was from another planet.

She wanted to hear the alien talk about space. He'd had so much of it. Light years and light years of black space to whiz around in.

"It must be like the freeway," she prompted him. "Except with no cars."

The alien nodded, then frowned. "There's more traffic than there used to be."

He did a beautiful job on the paint, ocher with blue trim, the colors of the desert in the late afternoon. The night he finished, as they were sitting out under the stars, he asked if there were anything else he could do for her, or if he should be moving on.

"Maybe you could just be with me," she said, tracing the inside of his hand-shell with her finger. "I'm so happy with you."

The alien blinked and drew her to him by surrounding her with an electromagnetic field.

"Me, too," he whispered. "You know, I could've finished this whole job in just a couple of hours."

"But there's one thing I'm afraid of," she said weakly. "Everybody's warned me about it."

The alien dropped the electromagnetic field and the two of them fell back into their respective lawn chairs.

"The anal probe?" he sighed.

She nodded, eyes popping out of her head. Everyone she knew who'd had an alien encounter – except for the Sheriff, who carried a gun – had been subjected to an anal probe. She didn't really understand why a crackerjack team of alien scientists would travel millions of light years to perform that particular exploratory surgery, but her neighbors' descriptions were too vivid to dismiss.

"Is the anus the key to human civilization?" she asked.

"You tell me," the alien said. "I've never seen one."

Reassured, she took him inside. They lay down on the airbed in the living room and took off all of their clothes. The alien was an ectomorph, with a narrow, concave chest. She was an ectomorph, too, so at least they had that in common. She tried to see if the alien's sexual organs resembled the ones in her dreams, but as soon as she laid a hand on him, his entire body gave off a bright green light that obscured her vision.

Lying there wondering what to do, how to pleasure an alien, she suddenly realized that this was how he was going to make love to her, with light. As he waved his shell-hands over her, she didn't feel more clitorises and vaginas form, instead she felt every cell in her body explode with pleasure. It was like shooting up oxycontin, the way her neighbor with the cereal box fence had described it. She felt so stupid. Of course that was what sex with an alien would be like – drugs.

Afterwards, she wondered if the alien had gotten anything out of it, but was afraid to ask. He'd spent most of his time playing with her ear, caressing it, licking it, burying his little alien nostrils in it. "What is this?" he cried out at one point, as his body light turned from green to gold. "Is this your anus?"

"No, no!" she said, alarmed. "It's my ear!"

"Aaaaah!" the alien groaned, and fell back on the airbed.

She did have nice ears.

She and the alien spooned all night long, and whenever he got up to go to the bathroom, she would rest her cheek in the cold spot where his little alien body had been. She felt so close to him, she began to think he must be a woman. After all, he'd never said he was a man, she'd merely deduced that from the windbreaker and the ski cap. But women wear windbreakers and ski caps, too. Some women. The ones who know how to fix things.

"Hey," she said softly, hugging his protruding rib cage. As it turned out, the alien was all bones. "Are you a man or a woman?"

The alien looked confused. "I don't understand the question."

For a week after that they did nothing but have sex. She could only imagine the light show her neighbors were getting. But on the eighth day she deflated the airbed and put it away.

"I need to know if we have a future together."

The alien looked sad. "Maybe in some other universe."

"Why not right here, right now?"

"Because your future lies with people, not aliens. Your planet is in serious trouble, but it's the only atmosphere you can survive. You all need to get together and find a way forward."

"Who cares about that stuff?" she cried, puddling. "You're my special someone! My *extra*-special someone!"

The alien stared out the screen door at a tarantula sidling by. "I can't stay. You know that."

"So then go," she said, flailing. "Just go!"

"I can't just go." The alien's huge black eyes filled with tears. "You have to help me."

In the end she was more than human to the alien, because the alien had been more than human to her. She made it an appointment with the Alien Contact Society up at Giant Rock, and gave it some cash.

"Think of them as an interplanetary travel agency," she said, when it didn't want to take her money.

The alien thanked her, looking deep into her eyes. "I'll never forget my time here with you."

She stuck out her chin. "Is that what you said to the nice lady down in Yucca Valley?"

"Aw," the alien said, surrounding her one last time with an electromagnetic field. "Don't be like that."

She started to weep. "Who will surprise me when you're gone?"

"You'll surprise yourself," the alien said. It was weeping, too, big purple tears that splashed onto the orange sofa and stained it green.

She didn't believe it at the time, but she did surprise herself after the alien went away. She lived on her own for a very long while, and was not bored or lonely or disappointed in humankind. On the contrary, she suddenly found herself interested in everything and everyone around her. She started attending community meetings down in Yucca Valley and helped run a superstore out of town. She joined a group that set up emergency water stations for migrants. She worked to reduce her carbon footprint and sent away for a solar oven.

She didn't share her alien encounter with her neighbors, because now that she'd had one of her own, she could tell they were making theirs up, but she still loved to listen to their stories. And she was always happy to go over and inspect the "evidence" – blistering scars, broken headlights, a carton of eggs splattered on the kitchen floor. Strange tracks like the imprint of a clothes iron in the sand. Power lines that hummed a little too loudly. Blurry snapshots of golden orbs zooming through the black desert sky.

5
THE MAKING OF *WILD CHILD*

Maria

I'd stopped writing for the day – which is to say, erased the one paragraph I had – and was watching the sunset from my motel window when a silver car pulled into the parking lot and drifted to a stop. The motor continued to run, for the air conditioning, I assumed, although no driver was visible through the tinted windows. The motor continued to run and the sun continued to set, the sky turning silver like the car, the car turning purple like the sky, until it wasn't hot anymore and the motor turned off.

Ten minutes later, a black car screeched into the lot and bumped to a stop next to the silver one, rocking back and forth. The driver of the black car got out right away. He was a short, bald man of about fifty, gnomish, yes, there was a restless energy about him, how to put it – charm, he had charm. He lit a cigarette and sucked on it like he needed it, rolled his eyes around the parking lot, leaned against his dusty car, looked up at the sky. Looked up at the sky as if it were any old evening sky, which it wasn't – it was the Mojave sky, bruised by L.A. pollution and scratched all over by planes and satellites, its silver scars still visible in the fading light. Then he looked down at the dirt like it was any old dirt, which it wasn't, the dirt here is light and powdery and it rises into the air when you put your foot down. Finally, he noticed the silence, there's no way to ignore that in this desert valley, it's a primeval non-noise, like the very first quiet and the very last.

"Baby?" he whimpered, and maybe she heard him, or maybe that was just the moment she picked to make her entrance, kicking the door of the silver car open with one long jeaned leg. She stayed like that for a while, one foot on the ground, not talking, until Lindy came out of the office and introduced herself.

Lindy
Strange couple, and I don't mean because she was tall, and he was kind of on the little side – that's a combination that works sometimes, me and Grady's like that and physically it's, well, a fit. No, strange because on the one hand they really seemed to get each other, and on the other hand they didn't seem to get each other at all. Usually the couples I see, and you see a lot of couples in the motel business, either don't understand each other and have made an agreement to just get on with it anyway, or – and this is rare – understand each other down to their very foot bones or at least think they do, or – and this is the case with new couples – are still learning about each other, with every meal, every walk, every drive to every destination, and still thinking that whatever they don't understand yet, they will someday soon. I don't know what kind of a couple I am with Grady. Maybe all three. But those two, they were in a different place. Which one had the idea to come out to Movietown in the middle of July, I'll never know, but it seemed like a funny setup for a couple on the rocks.

Maria
They followed Lindy inside and I pulled my curtains shut and switched on the lights. Company. Didn't want it. I'd been the only one staying at the motel for over a week, it was why I came there in the summer, to be the only one. The locals left you alone, and I was in no need of a here-we-are-in-the-desert camaraderie with fellow Angelenos. I knew I was in the desert. I'd been there for some time.

It was my grief counselor who suggested I come out here to begin with. The grief counselor I kept seeing for years and years after the event I was supposedly grieving for. The event the health plan deemed it necessary to grieve for and insure against, as opposed to all of the other events that came before and after. In the right light, what event isn't worth grieving? One's marriage, one's schooling, one's origins. That's the wrong light, my grief counselor used to tell me. That's why I kept going to her, because she saw things in shades. Here is the right light, according to her. She thought the desert was a fine place to be alone.

She also thought I might start writing again if I came out here. Therapists always propose that to me as a solution. Writing is not a solution, I tell them, writing is the putting into words of a problem. Exactly! they say, as if that were a solution. I have no special powers, I say. I am just a fifty-year-old woman with a silver bob. Don't attribute wisdom to me. Don't admire my crisp white blouses and my good posture. I am a failure of a human being. But you write books! they say, as if that were not a failure.

Lindy

Yeah, we're a team now, Grady and me, for better or worse, but I was running the Movietown Motel and Saloon on my own for three years before he came along. Bought it cheap from the last owner with the money Pop left me, pretty much all the money he had, which didn't sit too good with my brothers but they don't live around here anymore anyway – haven't for a long time.

Movietown was a set to begin with, built back in the forties when westerns were popular. It's supposed to look like a frontier Main Street in 1880. The studio put in a saloon at one end of the street and a motel across from that for the actors and crew, because there was no other type accommodation for twenty miles. They must've filmed about two hundred westerns here and then in the late sixties that all came to an end and it stood empty for over twenty years, until the guy I bought it from got title and fixed it up as a tourist attraction that never really got off the ground. He couldn't get people to come out, he told me, and when he got them to come out, he couldn't get them to come back. He figured it was just a little too kooky for most folks, because there was something here once but there wasn't ever anything here really.

But that's where I saw Movietown's potential – it was a place where people could come to make up their own stories. Pretend they were living in the Wild West or pretend they were starring in a western movie – these days what's the difference anyway?

When I bought the place I had the facades restored and re-painted along the street – the JAIL and the BANK and the SCHOOL-HOUSE and the SADDLERY. Put up the historic plaques, fixed the split rail fences. Got some old bargain ponies for the corral. Hired a band – the one Grady sings for now. Made a website.

And then I just sat, for close to three years. Out on the saloon verandah, where you can see all the way down the street and up into the hills. Got some local business, but no more than there'd ever been before. Mostly I just sat here, day after day, wondering what I'd done.

Which is how I happened to see Grady come in. He came in on a horse, if you can believe that, right there at the top of the street, came over the mountain and down through there where the sign says OK CORRAL. A bony white horse and he was even bonier, a little guy, like I said, with a nasty old yellow mustache that hung down to here and a tattered straw hat. Clopped right up to the porch, gave me that wide-open smile and that was it. Even when I found out he was a foot shorter than me, even when I found out he'd just gotten out of San Quentin, even when he told me – and he told me everything right up front – those two big saddlebags were full of marijuana, his grubstake, he called it, I didn't change my mind. Couldn't change my mind. My mind was gone.

His buddies started coming around when they found out where he was – bikers mostly, which was okay by me because bikers are the nicest ex-cons you'll ever know. Some hippies, too, and rock climbers – Grady had a lot of customers and all of them got along, more or less. The locals didn't have much choice but to get along, since we're still the nearest eat and drink for twenty miles. Then one day that author lady rents out a room and the next weekend some movie people come to stay and a couple of musicians after that, and before you know it, we got a reputation back in L.A. "The Fake Western Town that Became a Real Western Town," was the headline in the *Los Angeles Times* lifestyle section.

And like Grady says, all I had to do was get it on with an outlaw.

Maria

They came into the saloon later that night, the couple from the parking lot, but it was clear they weren't there to have a good time. They were there to avoid a bad time. He started chatting with the locals at the bar, but she went straight for a table in the corner and kicked out her long jeaned legs, staring in the direction of the band.

That's when I realized who she was. Fifteen years before she'd been one of those alty-indie-it-girl actresses, the ones they always use that French word to describe – *gamine.* She still sported her signature long shaggy bangs, but they were longer and shaggier now, less of an affectation and more of a deliberate withdrawal from view.

Twenty minutes later, he was still at the bar, postponing the next round in a fight that looked to be days if not weeks or years old, that evening round that knocks you out until morning, which is why he didn't see what the rest of us saw, the thing that made her and me and the band and Lindy gasp and turn to one another – wha? – not even knowing how to round out the question. From all appearances, an animal in a red dress had entered through the door on one side of the stage, darted across in front of the band and exited out the other side. It wasn't a little dog dressed up for a joke, and it wasn't some freaked-out pitbull that had run through a clothesline, either – this animal was big and it was wearing that dress, really wearing it.

That was what was strange. That was what made me realize after the fact that it was not an animal, but a girl who moved like an animal. The band kept right on playing, although they consulted each other first – nods all round. After all, nothing had happened to stop the music.

Lindy

I suspected it when she came in on the band like that but later when I was cleaning up she turned over the garbage and I ran out the side door and saw her and then I was sure.

Pop told me about another one once, a girl about ten years old who used to hang around a bar he went to up in Wonder Valley back in the fifties. The people that ran that bar, Warren and Evelyn Allen, had a Wild West show, with rodeo stunts and rope tricks and singing and dancing, and they saw the opportunity right away. Took her in – which is to say, dragged her in, because that's what you gotta do, and billed her as the Wild Child.

Pop couldn't remember what her act was exactly – maybe she just streaked around the ring the way this girl streaked across the stage. Wild children love live music, he told me, it's the only time they want anything to do with regular humans. I asked him what else he remembered about Warren and Evelyn's girl and he said the one thing that stuck out to him was she didn't know how to laugh.

With this one, it was her knuckles that cinched it for me, and her knees – you could see them through the dress, which was mostly whole in the bodice, but shredded to pieces in the skirt. They were both – knees and knuckles – calloused hard as rock. She had to have been running on them like an animal – probably running with the coyotes, since we don't have wolves up here.

When I came outside she froze, holding her hands up near her face like paws. She acted like an animal but you could still see something human about her, and I don't mean the dress but the misery, she was a poor animal and a poor human at the same time, she was stuck somewhere, she was all alone. I'm talking about her body and the way she moved, not her face, which was hidden behind a mess of thick black hair. You've never seen hair that dirty and tangled up, you could read time into her hair, years since it was brushed. I moved closer, trying to see just how many, but one, two, three steps in her direction and she was across the service porch and gone.

Maria
They set out early the next morning to try to beat the heat, the actress and the gnome. I heard the door close behind them. They weren't even in the room right next to me, they were several doors down, but out here sound travels. Just a click and I was up for the day – I'd been lucky to get in a couple of hours. Not their

fault – if it hadn't been them it would've been something else: the air conditioner switching on, a mourning dove, a fly.

When I saw them next they were high up on the ridge, but even from far away I could tell he was out of his element, walking and talking as if he were following her down some stale corridor – as if he and she and that business of theirs were all that mattered. She, on the other hand, kept stopping to look around at the rocks and the cactuses and the Joshua trees, and appeared to be listening for something.

Was that how Steven and I had looked? Except with roles reversed: me always talking, spinning out my interminable if only's – if only we'd built a fence, with a lock on the gate, if only we'd bought one of those nets that stretches over the water and keeps things out of it, like bodies, if only we'd bought another house, a house with no pool, a house with a different mother inside, a different father, a house with a grandmother, someone with wisdom, someone who knew how quickly things can go from bad to worse to the worst thing possible to the simply unimaginable if you don't stay vigilant, a flash of emerald green (her swimsuit) in all that aquamarine, her long, red hair (if only we'd cut it) roped around the ladder's bottom rung, the mermaid look in her eyes (ancient) and the gentle eddy that made me think for one brief, magical moment, *she is breathing*.

Me walking and talking like that, and him always listening for a way out.

– Jesus, it's hot! Sharon, are you even listening to me? I thought we were trying to have a conversation.
– Yes, but this isn't it.
– What do you mean?
– This is the same conversation we always have.
– Well then you say something.
– What's that?
– Then you say something!
– No, what's that?
– What?
– That noise. Listen!

– Sounds like hooves.
– It's softer than hooves. Harder than feet. Look!
– Where?
– Over there!
– Over where?
– That dust cloud. Look! It's her!
– Who?
– See the red? Up at the crest?
– Shit, she's really moving!
– Roland, she's coming straight at us!
– Get down!

– Sharon, what the?
– I don't think she was really coming for us. I think she just lost her balance.
– Lost her balance?
– Got too much momentum going. Look at that incline!
– Are those coyotes?
– Where?
– Sort of criss-crossing down from the top – up there, three of them!
– See, they know how to do it.
– Was that really a girl? Is that what they said last night?
– The woman from the motel office said people abandon kids out here all the time.
– Jesus. I can't believe that, can you?
– I don't know.
– And then they get picked up by coyotes?
– It happens in other countries. I saw a show about a wolf child they found in India.
– But that's India. How long could she have been out here without anybody seeing her?
– A while, I bet. Over that ridge it's wilderness.
– Wilderness! Gimme a break. We're only two hours from L.A.
– I wonder, when they kicked her out of the car – say that's how it happened – did she walk away from the lights instead of towards them?

– You mean by mistake? Or on purpose?

– That's what I'm wondering. What her position is.

– Position?

– Vis-a-vis humans. How she feels about being abandoned.

– I'm sure she feels pretty shitty.

– Then why doesn't she turn herself in?

– Sharon, you make her sound like a criminal.

– Okay, then why doesn't she seek us out?

– Maybe she was, just now. Maybe we should've stood our ground.

Maria

I was sitting in my usual corner that night when she made a beeline for my table. The actress. Apparently she needed someone to talk to. I'm not usually the first one people seek out when they come into a bar – or the second or third, for that matter – I'm not young or jolly or even kind-looking. I'm stiff in a way that stiffens others, and I compensate for my nervousness by acting irritated. None of that seemed to bother the actress, though.

"You're a writer?" she asked, sitting down across from me. "That's what the motel lady said. You were in here last night and I asked about you. I'm Sharon. You're from L.A., right? But you come out here a lot? Is it always this weird? I have to tell you – I was walking up on the ridge today with my husband and that girl came charging down at us! The one from last night! We were as close to her as I am to you now!"

"No kidding," I said, pushing my chair back. She was a little too close to me.

"Do you believe in this wild child business?" she asked.

"It seems pretty self-evident to me."

"But how long can she have been living out there?"

"Hard to tell."

"Doesn't it interest you?"

"Not really," I lied.

My new friend Sharon pushed her hair out of her eyes, which were so round and blue you couldn't help but swim in them a little. I could see why she kept them covered.

"I'm splitting up with my husband," she said, staring at me intently.

"Oh?"

"I should've left him a long time ago."

"Just out of curiosity, have you told him?"

She laughed and the gnome looked over from the bar, surprised.

"Sorry," she said. "I tend toward dramatic pronouncements. I'm an actress."

"I know. I've seen your movies."

She stiffened, her mouth a frozen little o.

"Not all of them," I said. "The ones you did with Roland Varminski."

"Oh." She seemed relieved. "That's him," she said, jerking her head towards the bar.

Encouraged by this show of acknowledgement, the gnome drifted over and handed her a beer, which she took without looking at him. He nodded at me and I nodded back.

"Roland," he said gruffly.

I nodded. Look buddy, I wanted to say. Your wife came over to *me*.

"And you are?"

"Maria," I answered, equally gruffly. He started to ask me another question, but as luck would have it that was the moment the band started to play.

They were on their second set when the girl came in, this time through the back door. Grady was singing and everybody in the saloon was standing or sitting still, which meant we all saw her this time, including Roland. I'm not normally a fan of country music, but Grady has one of those raspy voices that makes you thirsty without knowing exactly what it is you're thirsting for, and when he really lets loose, which he was doing right then, you have no choice but to stop and think about it. It was in this moment of collective reflection that we saw the girl creeping along the wall towards the stage, feeling her way with long crooked fingers over the framed pictures of western stars that hung there. Grady kept on singing – I could see him make a conscious decision to continue – maybe he thought he was speaking to her, drawing her to him, I don't know, but it ended badly, with her crashing onto the stage, tipping over the drums and the drummer, a bearded biker with a serious center of gravity, which tells you how strong she was, and then leaping – there's no other way to put it – out the side door. Where she'd gone out a scrap of red fluttered from the latch, and somebody went over and got it and passed it around. It was a piece of her dress, rotten from the sun. After that, Lindy shut all the doors, and the band packed up their instruments and went to get drinks from the bar.

Roland tried to get Sharon to go back to the room with him but she wouldn't. Her eyes were bright, and she kept saying to no one in particular, "What a crazy scene!"

"Baby," he said, tilting his head meaningfully.

"You go ahead. I want to stay with Maria," she said, moving her chair closer and lacing her arm through mine. "We're just getting acquainted."

Roland shrugged and tossed a twenty down on the table.

"Don't believe a word she says, Maria," he said, winking at me. Couple games. It dawned on me that they were both drunk.

After Roland had gone, Sharon let go of my arm and spilled her guts. No surprises there. I could've written it myself: the long silent days in the empty-feeling house in Laurel Canyon, the ever-narrowing stream of scripts coming in for her (she was too identified with his films, plus she was now, in Industry parlance, a "mature actress") and checks coming in for him (his only job in a year a movie about a lacrosse team rape for Lifetime), the smashed avocados by the pool, thick thuds all night long, brown leaves in the water, who cared if they were going to have to sell it all soon anyway? Who cared if they were going to have to sell anyway, it wasn't the money that mattered. She spoke with the flat intonation of someone who's decided her life is shit, and though I ached to say, you think your life is shit, I restrained myself, because, as my grief counselor used to say when I brought up massacres in Rwanda, suffering isn't relative, it's cumulative.

So I held my tongue and Sharon went on and on in that funny flat voice, not even noticing the drunk Marine prowling around our table. He was pretty hard to miss – stumbling, even bumping into us sometimes, or me, anyway, since he was staring at her and that requires a little distance. He'd been staring at her all night, not like he was screwing up his nerve to approach her, not like he even dreamed of it – no, he was memorizing her face, not to tell his buddies about, either, it wasn't that kind of thing, more likely to take with him the next time he got shipped out to that other desert, to have before him when his world exploded or he exploded somebody else's, his own private Angel of Mercy. Add that to everything else that had already happened that evening and perhaps you'll forgive me for excusing myself to go to the bathroom and then ducking out the side door. The night was black and the stars were out and a screech owl followed me across the dusty road to my room, flitting from post to post.

Lindy

It was my idea to bring her in. I told Grady I couldn't have her coming through tearing up the place and bothering the customers, and he says Lindy honey I don't think you know what you're getting into and I say don't Lindy honey me and he says why're you getting so bent outta shape and I say Grady I don't ask much. He says, well what're you going to do with her once we get a hold of her, you can't turn her over to Child Welfare think what'll happen to her, and I say, I was thinking of raising her myself. And Grady looks at me for a long time and then shakes his head and says this is beyond me.

I had a dream the night she climbed up onstage and knocked over Big Jim that made me want to do it. I'd never wanted kids. I nursed my dad for so long, first through the diabetes, then through the cancer, that when it was all over I never wanted to nurse anyone again. I was up front about all that with Grady in the beginning and he said, don't worry Lindy, when I go it'll be in a gunfight and the other guy will be DEA and the better shot.

But in the dream I was brushing her hair with a silver-backed brush, and she was sitting there like a little lamb, wearing the hairband I'd made her out of a white satin ribbon, the way Mama used to do me on Sunday mornings. They cut my hair short after she died and I've always worn it like this so it doesn't need tending, but the girl's hair was long and soft and I could tell she was grateful to have it brushed. I couldn't see her face but she was leaning back into me in a way that seemed grateful or at least like she was enjoying herself and I was enjoying myself and leaning forward into her.

When I woke up from the dream, that's when it hit me, how wrong it all was, wrong to leave her out there with the coyotes, wrong to shut the doors on her so she couldn't hear the music, wrong to act like she was more of an animal than a human. And right away it hit me, too: I wanted her for my little girl, and I wanted to name her Cathy. Cathy was Mama's name and it's what Pop started to call me at the end, just before he died, when I guess it seemed like anything was possible again.

Maria

Sharon didn't turn up at the saloon the next night, but Roland did, and sidled up to me while I was eating the dried-out chicken and mealy fries that go by the name of "dinner platter" in Movietown.

"How's your food?"

I waved my hand over the plate. "I think it speaks for itself."

"Mind if I sit down?" he said, sitting down. "Sharon's not feeling so hot. I want to bring something back to her."

"Well, don't bring her this."

"She says you're a writer."

"I have been."

"What kind?"

"Fiction."

"Give me some titles."

"I seriously doubt you would know them."

"Try me. What's your last name?"

"Jensen."

"Maria Jensen?"

"Yes."

"Maria Jensen?"

"Yes, Maria Jensen, why?"

"I optioned one of your novels is why! Five – no ten years ago now!"

"You did?"

"Didn't you know?"

"My agent used to handle all of that."

Roland was silent, giving the phrase "used to handle" due consideration.

"I liked it a lot," he said, after a moment. "It was about a war correspondent. Not sensationalist at all – very subtle, very moving. Of course I couldn't get any studio to make it."

"Of course," I said brightly. "But now you have a gig at Lifetime?"

He grimaced and shifted in his chair.

"She told you that, huh?"

"She mentioned it in passing."

"Sharon used to star in my movies, you know – the good ones, early on. A few times there we really clicked."

"I think I saw those times," I said.

Roland smiled sadly. How nice if the conversation could end right here, I thought, but of course it couldn't.

"Working on any new projects?" he said.

"Not to speak of."

"But you were good!"

I shrugged and started back in on my chicken. "I lost interest."

Roland laughed and flagged down the waitress. "On that note," he said, pointing to my plate, "two of those to go."

Not such a bad guy, I thought, when he'd gone. At least he hadn't said, "Whatever happened to you?" the way they usually did. Whatever happened to you, as if you weren't standing right there in front of them.

– Sharon?

– Hmm?

– How's the hangover?

– Hmm? What're you doing?

– Can I just sit here? I brought you dinner.

– Not hungry. What're you looking at? Don't look at me like that.

- Sorry.
- Last night was a mistake.
- It was?
- Yes. Eat yours over there.

- There was talk in the bar about that wild child.
- What kind of talk?
- I guess they're trying to figure out a way to catch her.
- Why would they want to do that?
- Sounds like she's becoming a nuisance. She stole some fresh meat out of the kitchen at lunchtime, right off the counter. And they think she killed the cook's cat. And ate it.
- What?
- Well, she has been living with coyotes.
- What're they going to do with her?
- Someone said the motel lady wants to adopt her.
- Why don't they just leave her alone?
- Sharon. She can't be more than seven or eight years old.
- I guess, but it sounds dangerous.
- For her or for them?

- Sharon?
- What?
- Are you falling asleep?
- No.
- Because I was thinking I might videotape it. I don't think a real wild child has ever been caught on film. Truffaut, Herzog – those were actors, weren't they?
- You caught me on film. I was almost a child and I was wild.

Lindy

So Grady, bless 'im, got the bikers together and told them the deal, and then they, bless 'em, put their heads together and came up with the idea to throw a net over her. Sometimes the simplest plan is the best. But first we had to figure out a way to get her back into town. I had the idea to set up a big mirror down at the end of Main Street because they say wild children are fascinated by their reflection – not that they recognize themselves, they think they see another creature inside there trying to communicate with them. I don't know, maybe that's what it is to recognize yourself. Warren Allen tried it on his girl one time, and she sat frozen for hours, staring.

So that's what we did, in the morning we laid a mirror up against the sidewall of the JAIL, which is at the very end of the street, next to the OK CORRAL. I wanted to do it down there so as not to bother the customers, but the customers all seemed to be out there anyway, and that director was filming it with his camcorder. Me and Big Jim and some of the other guys hid around the corner, ready with the net, and Grady stood out in front of the JAIL, strumming his guitar and singing. I'd never heard him sing that way before, didn't know he had it in him, but I guess back before the drugs and the jail time he had one of those beautiful clear voices, and he can still get it back when he sings softly. Grady always told me he was a choirboy but I never believed it until right then. I almost went to him myself, his singing was so beautiful, almost went and laid down at his feet.

I guess the wild child wasn't as impressed, though, because she never showed up. We stayed out there until noon without so much as a rustle in the bushes, and then it just got too damn hot. I felt like my brain was microwaving, cooking from the inside, Grady's throat was closing up from the dust and the bikers' beer was at a boil. The only one who yelped when we called it a day was the director.

I left the mirror out there just in case but back at the saloon everybody agreed it looked like she'd gotten wise to us and we needed another plan. Some people even started saying she'd split for good. She was just here yesterday, I said, maybe a little too loud, and Grady patted my hand.

Maria
The next night Roland and Sharon came into the saloon together, and they were drunk and careless. Maria, Maria, do you always come here by yourself? Maria, where do you live in L.A? Do you live alone? Do you like that, Maria? Living alone?

"Looks like you two are getting along," I said, and that seemed to shut them up, but it turned out they were just gathering their strength.

How come you won't answer our questions? they came back with. You think we're obnoxious Hollywood types, is that right? We're not really, you know, New York is our real home.

And then it was back to me:

HIM
Are you nursing a broken heart, Maria?

HER
That's really why you're hiding out here, isn't it?

HIM
Come on, lay it on us, we've laid plenty on you. Who was he?

HER
Or her?

HIM
Come on, tell us, don't be shy! Who broke your heart?

HER
(giggling)
Tell us, Maria. Let it out. Who?

ME
Who broke my heart? All of you. The whole damn lot of you.

HIM AND HER
All of us?

ME
Yes, all of you, with your questions and your problems and your frailty and your bullying and your kindness and your ambition and your fear and your manipulations and your certitude and

your doubt and your self-loathing and your arrogance and your generosity and your good intentions and your bad intentions and your predictability and your singularity and your awkwardness and your grace and your stories and your hopes, your hopes, it breaks my heart that you still have them.

I stopped, although I wasn't finished, and looked down at the table. End of scene.

But no – one, two, three beats and then their eyebrows came down and I looked up and everything kept going, only a little more quietly and gently than before. Sharon smiled wistfully at me from under her shaggy bangs, and Roland ordered another round of beers. After all, nothing had happened to stop the music.

Lindy
Two days later, we caught her. I'm not proud of what we did, but it seemed necessary at the time. There were so many things she needed, now that I'd started to think about it. For one, a bath. And underwear and shoes and a new dress, a couple of new dresses. And a bedroom of her own. And schooling.

The way it happened – I heard a noise out in back of the saloon, heard it over or under the music, I don't know how I heard it but I waved my arms at Grady and pointed to the door and the band stopped playing and Big Jim got the net and we all lined up against the inside wall. Big Jim shoved the director and his camcorder out of the way and quieted everybody down and then Grady pushed the door open softly and there she was, batting at the padlock I'd put on the garbage shed after that first night like a cat with a mouse, so concentrated she didn't even hear us at first, and we were able to feed the net to Grady and Big Jim and they were able to jump out and throw it over her.

Right away she started twisting and snarling, it took four of the guys to wrestle her to the ground and all four came out with cuts on their arms and necks – nasty cuts that were blue around the edges. It took those four and another three to get her down Main Street and into the soundstage, a big old wooden warehouse in back of the SCHOOLHOUSE that hadn't been used since the movie days, and it's hard to describe how they looked at the end of that. Cut up and bruised, but something else besides – they looked shaken to the core, the way folks look after a fire or an earthquake. The way she fought, they couldn't get over that, every foot of the way, except for the last twenty or so when they outright dragged her, and they couldn't get over that, either.

They put her inside the soundstage and barred the door, and then we all just stood there listening to her race around inside, you could hear her nails clicking on the concrete – it's four thousand square feet in there, so she had plenty of room. Every now and then we heard a thud somewhere in the distance and then a little grunt. She was testing out the walls. Once she banged into the door and we all jumped back, but it held.

She's secured, Grady said, and that made me happy. I asked him when he thought she'd be ready for visitors and he said maybe in the morning, although he looked like he had his doubts.

Maria

This time it was Sharon who came to get dinner for Roland.

"Not that he'll even touch it."

"Is he sick?"

"No," she said, rolling her eyes. "He's making a movie."

"What do you mean?"

"He's been playing his video footage of the Wild Child's capture over and over again for hours now, looking for The Shot.

"The Shot?"

"He wants a close-up, but she moves around too much. She's a blur."

"That could be interesting, too. A blur."

"That's what I told him, but he wants her in focus." Sharon shook her head and smiled. "It's good to seem him like this actually."

"Like what?"

"So – attentive. That was what drew me to Roland in the first place – his attention."

"Uh huh."

"I don't mean just to me, to everything. He was fascinated by the world back then. The texture of it, every little detail. I found that so attractive."

"Uh huh."

She laughed. "Were you always brokenhearted, Maria? Even as a kid?"

"Especially as a kid. Were you always gorgeous?"

She shrugged. "I started modeling when I was nine months old. My dad left and my mom needed a way to support us."

"How long did you do that for?"

"A long time. I was lucky not to have zits. Got my first big cosmetics campaign when I was fourteen. To celebrate my mom redid my room as a surprise. What a surprise. When I left for the shoot that morning it was just a normal girl's room in a house on Long Island – well, it was just my room– but when I came back that evening..." Sharon waved her hand around to indicate mental instability. "My mother said it was the room she'd always wanted me to have, the room that I deserved."

It wasn't hard to imagine that new room – the fine lace of her mother's hopes, the chintz of her expectations, the massive armoire of her determination. We've all opened the door to that room at least once, but to have to live there, Sharon said, was too much, and her senior year of high school she fled Long Island for Manhattan on the back of her drug dealer's Harley.

"Not long after that, I met Roland – a punky film school student with a receding hairline and this vein in his forehead that throbbed whenever he got excited – and we started making movies. And for a few years there – ten years even – it felt like I was really living. We were really living. Making people see the world the way we saw it, and not the other way around."

"So what happened?'

She shrugged. "I guess Roland got scared."

"Of what?"

"Of risking it. Being on the outside again. Losing what he had." She twisted her mouth to the side. "And then he started up with the girls."

"Ah, the girls."

"And then I left. And then I came back. And now here we are."

"Whose idea was it to come out here?"

"Mine. It seemed like a good place for a showdown."

"High Noon?"

"Something like that. But instead I'm here talking your ear off and Roland's shut up in our room making a movie."

"About a girl shut up in a soundstage."

"To the Wild Child!" Sharon polished off her beer and thumped the mug down on the table. "Enough about me. Enough about Roland. Let's go see about her."

"Rather not," I said, but she pulled me to my feet.

"Just to where we can see the building," she said. "You don't have to go any further."

"I'd really prefer – "I began, but we were already at the door. I stepped outside. What harm could it do to go look at the sound-stage? It was a beautiful night. The heat had dissipated and the air was soft and liquid feeling as we trudged along, the summer-dried grass snapping under our feet.

We were almost there when a howl came from inside the building – or no, it wasn't that coherent, it was more of a splattered sound, a yelping or a yammering, that noise that coyotes make. We both stopped in our tracks when we heard it, but it was Sharon who noticed the line of yellow eyes on the hill above us. Squinting, I could just make out the shadowy bodies of the pack: small, malnourished, like an army battalion at the end of a very long war, all young boys and old men.

"I wonder why they don't respond," Sharon said.

"Perhaps she's contaminated for them now. They probably see her as human."

"I think it's because they're ashamed. They want to help her but there's nothing they can do."

She might've had something there. It's true, the coyotes didn't answer the girl's cry, but nor did they slink away. When we turned back towards the motel we could still see the outline of the pack on the hillside wavering.

Lindy

Now it was my turn to creep along a wall. There was a heap at the far end of the soundstage, I could see that, but I couldn't see much more. It was still dark out. I'd wanted to come before Grady woke up because I knew he would stop me. I'd wanted to come before she woke up, too. I thought I could get nearer that way, and I did.

She was lying on her side with her legs and arms stretched out in front of her. I could see her twitching, running in her sleep. I wanted to get close enough to see her eyes moving under the lids, too, to see her eyelashes – I bet she had beautiful eyelashes, long and thick and curly, and a button nose and a sweet sharp little chin under all that crazy hair.

I don't know what my plan was, I didn't really have a plan beyond touch. I wanted her to know what it was like to feel a hand, to feel fingers. I wanted to sing Careless Love to her, the way Mama always did to me. The long, soft hair, the white ribbon would come later, after the touch and the voice.

But I didn't get a chance to know if I had healing hands or not, because she woke up when my hand was six inches away from her face and did what I guess came natural to her – she bit it. I jumped back and that set her off racing around the warehouse, it seemed like everywhere I turned she was there – I could feel her, the wind from her, although it was still too dark to see more than a few feet in any direction – so I tucked my head down and waited. It was instinct, I felt like she was going to come for my eyes next, I don't know why. The strange thing was how quiet it was, neither one of us making a sound.

Eventually I turned back towards the door and saw daylight there around the edges, and that's when I knew that it was my eyes that were going to save me, my eyes and my legs, because my hands and arms were useless, one cradling the other, funny how things break down in that kind of situation, you're not a whole person anymore just a collection of parts and some parts are the victims and other parts are the heroes and you're sort of outside of the action, egging them on. When I got to the door, just before I slipped out and barred it behind me with my elbow – she could've done that, too, if she'd known – I looked down and saw the tray of food I'd put there the night before, untouched.

Grady took me down to the Medical Center in town to get fixed up and when we got back the bikers were all lined up in front of the soundstage. Grady told me he put them there to keep anyone else from getting hurt but I know he gave them orders first and foremost to keep me out because they started kicking at the dirt when they saw me coming – as if to say, aw come on, Lindy, don't make us. So I started whistling to keep it casual and walked on past them to the motel office to ice my hand and think of another way in.

Maria

The next day, all day, the area around the soundstage was a circus, mostly due to Roland's presence – or rather, the presence of Roland's video camera, which encouraged a certain exhibitionism. From my perch on the saloon verandah (empty except for me), I could see the bikers sprawled out in front of the entrance, their pirate beards spread out over their barrel chests – "guarding" the soundstage, they said, although Roland couldn't get them to say from what or whom. Twenty or thirty locals were standing around in straw hats and visors, and the band was there too picking out some tunes, because musicians will go anywhere there's a crowd and a carnival feeling, even if it is a hundred degrees. And then there was Grady standing to one side, brooding over something, and Sharon standing to the other side, brooding over something else, and Lindy, who only came through at mealtimes. That was a somber moment, when Lindy stuck her hands through the door and pulled out the full tray and put another full tray back in its place.

As for inside the soundstage, it was totally silent now, no more howling or yowling or whatever it was Sharon and I had heard the other night. The coyotes had disappeared, and they didn't even come back when it got dark and the bikers rolled out their sleeping bags.

I hold Roland responsible for the news cameras that showed up the following day too, since he was the one who gave people the idea that this was a media event. Somebody must have called it in. Once the news trucks showed up, the crowd tripled in size and the bikers actually had to stand up and form a ring around the soundstage, because people kept trying to get a look at the girl through the holes in the boards.

I ordered a sandwich in the saloon and took it back to my room to avoid the lunchtime rush. On the way there I met Roland returning from his room with a fresh battery for the camera.

"Getting pretty crazy out there," I said.

"It's fantastic! You won't believe the shots I'm getting. There are some real actors in this crowd. Especially those bikers."

"But Sharon says you're still waiting for The Shot?"

Roland frowned. "I haven't been able to get close enough."

"Do you need to get that close?"

"I want to see her eyes. Don't you?"

"Yes and no."

"I tell you what I really want to see. I want to see her laugh."

"That might be hard to accomplish under the circumstances."

"The motel lady told me they never laugh, in fact."

"Who?"

"Wild children."

"It's impossible then, the shot you want."

He chewed his lip and I could see the throbbing vein in his forehead that had first endeared him to Sharon. "I guess it depends on how wild she really is. Or how funny we really are."

Lindy

Okay, so we didn't know what we were doing, I'll admit that, we didn't have a plan yet – well, Grady had a plan, Grady's plan was to set her loose, but I hadn't agreed to it. But we sure as hell had a better idea of how to handle the situation than Child Welfare.

I saw the woman get out of her car from the motel office window. As soon as I saw that outfit – the black jacket, the red pants, the bun, the clipboard – I knew she was coming from an office, and there was only one office that was going to be interested in what was happening out here. I jumped up and went out to greet her, intercepted her, you might say, before she could find her way around to Main Street.

Hi, she says, and right away asks me if I've seen a little girl wandering around. No ma'am, I say, there's nobody here this time of year – hardly any customers at all. This little girl was abandoned, she says, and I say, abandoned? What a crying shame! Nothing like that around here. Somebody called it in? Well that's a crying shame, too, making you come all the way up here for a hoax.

Then she asks me about my hand, what happened to it, and I say, oh, don't be alarmed by the bandage, it's almost healed now. Lost my charm bracelet and went looking through the garbage for it, cut my hand on a can of beans, can you beat that?

She wrote some things down on her clipboard, and that was going to do it, I knew that was going to do it, because I'd had dealings with Child Welfare before, after Mama died and my brothers split and the neighbors called in that Pop wasn't looking after me. A social worker came by then too, but she didn't look too hard either. She already had more cases than she could handle. She sort of signaled it to us, the way she stared out the window – if we didn't want to tell her, she didn't really need to know.

So this one is on her way back out to the parking lot, and I'm walking with her just to make sure she keeps facing in the right direction when all of a sudden she spins, that's right, spins on her heel, so clean I figure she had to be on the drill team in high school, she spins and she stops and she points over the roof of the motel office. What's that? she says.

Looks like some kind of crane, I say. TV antenna? You think so? Sure, sure thing you can go look, I'll go with you. Okay, and maybe I should let you in on some things on the way over. Didn't want to bother you is all, I know how busy you folks are at Child Welfare.

Yeah, I was wrong, dead wrong about her – I guess we got the one lady social worker with some pep left in her step because she was fit to be tied when she saw the crowd out on Main Street and found out we had the girl. I'm taking her with me right now, she says to Grady, tell your men to let me through, and when Grady tries to reason with her she says, I'm trained to handle children. She's not a child exactly, Grady says, she's part animal too, and that really sends that social worker over the top. Let me by, she yells and we do, because she's the Law or anyway closer to the Law than any of us.

Maria
I watched the whole thing unfold that afternoon from the saloon verandah – lunchtime was over and everyone else had returned to the scene, so I was once again the only one sitting out there. It was a strange way to see it happen, because what I was seeing was a sound, but I didn't know that at first. The wind must've been blowing the other way.

Anyway, this what I saw: I saw the woman in the red pants push past Grady into the soundstage, I saw Roland try to follow her and the drummer shove him out of the way, I saw the door shut behind her, and then I saw everybody listening. A minute later, I saw a ripple spread through the crowd – a sort of group cringe. I saw some people start forward and some people step back, I saw the news reporters and the camera people spin out from their little circles to stare, then turn back to gather up their equipment, and I saw Lindy standing stock still, as if she'd been turned to stone. It was only then that I finally heard something, only then that the wind shifted and the sound came to me, a woman's scream, although it's possible I'd been hearing it all along.

Lindy
Grady took the Child Welfare lady down to the Medical Center and they said she was going to need to have surgery. She was bitten and scratched in multiple places, including her eye, and her shoulder was dislocated. Your wife was lucky, they told him – that bite on her hand was nothing compared to this. When Grady told me that I didn't have the right reaction – I smiled. I smiled because I thought it must mean something about the girl and me, about our connection. To tell you the truth, I smiled because I was sure it wasn't luck at all. I knew what it was like, see, to be let go, to be so dirty your fingers leave streaks on your school books. And I knew too what it was like to feel better around animals than people, to spend your days trying to get close to chipmunks and jackrabbits and lizards and doves, because animals have no past

and no future and can't poison themselves with remembering or imagining. It was only for a couple of months, right after Mama died, Pop stopped drinking after that and never touched the bottle again, but it was long enough to know.

Then Grady started yelling at me, saying we had to set the girl loose, we had at most a couple of days before the social worker got out of the hospital and Child Welfare got the story straight and came back for her. And I told him if he did that then it was over between us, because if he did that then I'd never get her back. Well, what's your plan, he said, and I said my plan is to sit myself outside of that soundstage and make sure none of you do what you think is best for me.

So I did what I said, I got a chair from the office and sat down in front of the door to the soundstage. The guys all looked over at Grady for direction but he just shrugged and walked away.

Maria
Less than twenty-four hours later they came back for the girl – four Sheriff's deputies and two more county employees from Child Welfare. This time only Lindy blocked the door, the bikers melted into the crowd as soon as they saw law enforcement.

Child Welfare must've been warned about Lindy, or let's say informed, because the social workers smiled and spoke to her very gently, one of them even called her softly by name, and she stared at him and nodded, although she didn't appear to be tracking. They talked to her for a good fifteen minutes and then Grady put his arm around her and moved her away from the door, and the deputies went right in, followed by the social workers. I looked around for Roland and sure enough, there he was, sneaking into position in front of the news cameras so that he could get The Shot when they all came back out.

This time there was no sound, inside or out, I was standing right there in the middle of the crowd and you could've heard a pin drop. A few minutes later the deputies came out and said something to Grady and Lindy, who gasped, and a moment later the social workers came out empty-handed and everyone else gasped too.

"Cathy!" Lindy screamed. "Cathy! Cathy!" She tore away from Grady and ran inside the soundstage, with Roland following close behind.

Roland was the first to emerge, shaking his head.

"What is it?" Sharon called out. "What happened to her?"

"Not there," Roland muttered, sitting down on the dusty ground and thumping his back up against the wall. "Gone."

They found blood in the crumbled concrete where she'd dug herself under and out, and a big section of the dress snagged on the boards, which meant that wherever she was now, she was practically naked. The Sheriff held a search that night and most of the crowd from the soundstage joined in, a hundred flashlights combing the hills – it was quite a show.

Lindy and Grady and some of the others stayed below, Lindy stroking a blanket, something to cloak the girl with if they found her, Grady stroking Lindy's hair the way they always do, it's the only thing they can think to do. It was a pitiful sight all right, and that little girl was never even Lindy's to begin with. They never are yours, that's the thing nobody tells you, from the day they're born you're always only borrowing.

Me, I went back to my room and pulled the curtains shut and turned the AC up loud. I knew they would never find her, she was gone, she'd chosen the desert over them. She obviously had no desire to take part in this human project of pulling things down out of the sky, things with wings, and turning them back into children. I had no desire to either, none left – no, not even to witness the spectacle – so I turned out the lights and went to sleep.

I saw Sharon and Roland as they were leaving the motel the next morning and we made a show of exchanging phone numbers and addresses. I'd thought they would be downcast by the recent turn of events, but to my surprise they were elated. They'd figured out a way to make the movie without The Shot.

Roland reached up and clasped Sharon around the waist. "It was her idea," he said with a grin. "She figured it out even before the girl disappeared."

Sharon smiled and winked at me from under her shaggy bangs. "Better that way really, given the subject."

Lindy and Grady took a little longer to work things out. The next few times I came out to Movietown, Grady was nowhere to be seen. But the time after that, he was back singing in the band, and the time after that Lindy was proudly carrying around their newly adopted daughter Cindy – or Cathy, maybe it was – a black-haired little girl rumored to be the love child of a lady Marine stationed in Afghanistan.

The movie *Wild Child* came out the following year to critical acclaim, and Roland and Sharon went on to make a series of documentaries together – all of them omitting The Shot. "Intentionally withholding the full picture," the *Los Angeles Times* critic said, "their films document the question and not the answer." For a while I toyed with the idea of calling up Roland and Sharon and letting them in on a little secret, but in the end I decided against it. Why mess up a good thing, their good thing? Especially since it was this little secret that gave me the idea for what might be – God forbid – my next story.

Remember the day they tried to get the girl to come down from the hills – the day of the mirror and Grady singing his sweetest song? Well, that evening, on the way back to my room from the saloon, I saw something move down at the end of the street, by the JAIL. I went to look – who wouldn't have? – but I hid behind the building and peered around the corner, afraid to get any closer than that.

Which is how I saw, not her face, because her hair fell forward, covering it, nor her reflection, because I was standing to one side of her, but the Wild Child gazing at her reflection in what must have been its terrible beauty: her half-animal, half-human, half-girl, half-boy, half-young, half-old, half-lost, half-found, half-in, half-out, weary, wary, wily, wise, ignorant, innocent, shivering, shimmering reflection, and how I saw her touch her long crooked finger to the cold hard glass and laugh.

6

WONDER VALLEY

OWENS, VICTORIA

Letter of Application

To the Wonder Valley Arts Foundation:

I am writing to apply for the Wonder Valley Artist's Residency, June–July 2004. Your description of Wonder Valley as "centrally located in the middle of nowhere" struck a chord with me, because I was centrally located in the middle of nowhere for many years– that nowhere being the art world. I have a feeling, though, that your nowhere is more of a somewhere than mine. I hope so, anyway.

Before I was in the thick of things, I think I made better art. Particularly ages eleven to twelve, in Yorkshire. But everything changed when, as a young adult, I experienced a staggering amount of fame. That was in London, ages twenty-three to twenty-five. Something I did (a big painting of a big ape) caused huge numbers of people to take notice of me. It didn't have to be an ape, it could've been a shark suspended in formaldehyde or a piece of elephant dung, but it just so happens it was an ape, reaching down from the heavens to touch the finger of God.

Suffice it to say that the process by which the ape painting – and I – became known to millions remains obscure to me. I mean, I understand it logistically – there was that flap with the Catholic League of Decency and then the giant advert in Piccadilly Circus with me reaching down from the heavens to touch a laptop computer – but existentially it exceeds my grasp. I only know that the experience shut me down creatively. In the years since, I have gradually become, like many an artist with a teething baby or an academic job, somebody who does not make work. I assume they are my primary competition for this residency in the middle of nowhere, which your literature says is specially designed for artists whose creative output has slowed or stopped. Believe me, I need it more than they do, because they have their babies and their academic jobs, and I have nothing. Oh, I made plenty of money back in the day, but I spent it all on lovers and designer clothes. And anyway, it's not money I'm after now, or fame. What I'm after is a new beginning.

Hence, a new medium. Though I am or have been a painter, for this project I would like to do a site-specific installation. My installation, "Tumbleweed Garden," will be a garden of tumbleweeds. Tumbleweeds tumbling, not growing out of the ground. I propose erecting a fence around an acre of land to corral them – a plexiglas fence so you can see them tumbling from afar. Perforated plexiglas, so the wind blows through.

Why tumbleweeds? Tumbleweeds tumble across land that is not cultivated or able to be cultivated – perhaps because it has suffered an environmental disaster such as nuclear testing. At a certain stage in the growth cycle, tumbleweeds separate from their roots and go into motion, carrying hundreds of thousands of seeds and dropping hundreds of them wherever they touch down. Tumbleweeds are dead but they continue to produce – more worthless tumbleweeds.

I believe my project has much to say about the contemporary art world and its relation to consumer culture and global capitalism. It has much to say about American hegemony in the post-Cold War era (a tumbleweed by any other name would be a Russian thistle). It has much to say about the rape of the land in the Wild West. I won't know exactly how much unless you help me make it.

I may not be able to paint at the moment, but a garden I can do. After I became famous and infamous – which turned out to be the same thing – I left England, disguised myself as an organic farmer, and hid out in New Zealand for several years. I know how to tend things.

But now I want to make art again, and I want to make it in the California desert. Please let me come to Wonder Valley.

Sincerely,

Victoria Owens

Letter of Acceptance

Dear Ms. Owens,

It is our great pleasure to offer you a June-July residency in Wonder Valley. Please be advised that you will be the only resident. This seemed to correspond to your needs, but we wanted to be sure. We are not like other artists' colonies. You will not make lifelong friends here, or have romantic escapades. Wonder Valley is something different.

As you know, the Wonder Valley Arts Foundation Artist's Residency is designed to stimulate production by artists who are creatively "blocked." This tends to be an American problem for some reason, but not always. We've been helping artists come unblocked since the seventies, and believe we've developed a pretty good mechanism. The setting itself does much of the work. We ask only that you keep a log of your project during your stay, and leave a copy for our files when your residency is over, along with any photo documentation. There are no other requirements. We will not be checking up on you during your stay.

You should know that the residence is not on the water line and the well sometimes goes out. If this happens, you may take a shower down at the Barking Coyote. The Barking Coyote is a bar, but there's a shower in back for people who aren't on the water line and a room with a bed for customers who've had too much to drive home (often the same people). It is located twenty miles from the artist's residence.

We've sectioned off an acre near the residence with wooden stakes and yellow police tape. This is the area reserved for "Tumbleweed Garden." Some time in your first week of residency, it is possible that a contractor by the name of Robert Dimmick will show up with an acre's worth of plexiglas and install the fencing you've requested. We say "it is possible" because unfortunately, although Mr. Dimmick is on the Wonder Valley Arts Foundation payroll, we cannot vouch for his arrival. He does not have a phone. You have a fifty-fifty chance of finding him at the Barking Coyote, if you catch my drift.

In this envelope, you will find keys and a stipend check, along with directions to the residence and the Barking Coyote. If you do choose to frequent the Barking Coyote, keep an eye out for a man they call Teacher. He is kind, and drinks a lot. He is a great supporter of the Wonder Valley Arts Foundation. He is not actually a teacher. Congratulations, and good luck to you.

Sincerely,

Wonder Valley Arts Foundation

Project Log

June 11, 2004
Arrived yesterday evening. The "artist's residence" is a caravan on forty acres of scrub. A clean caravan, thankfully. Christ, it's hot. Hot and dry. Feels like my bones are bleaching through my skin. Well water trickles through the faucets for the moment. Smelly well water. Walked out to the garden site. Bloody desolate. No sign of Mr. Dimmick No sign of a tumbleweed, either. Never thought they'd go for a project this daft, but they did and now I've actually got to make it. What was I thinking?

June 15, 2004

Late this afternoon, Robert Dimmick arrived with the plexiglas. It's yellow, not at all what I requested. I requested clear. "Piss Tumbleweed," I said, "that's what they'll call it." He told me it would take six more weeks for an acre's worth of clear plexiglas to arrive. "Bloody hell," I said. "Put up what you've got."

He managed to erect one side of the fence before dark, a short side. Dimmick is small and red-faced but strong, a fast worker, and I'm sure he can get it all up in two or three days. I asked him if he knew where I could find some tumbleweeds, but he said that was not his area of expertise.

June 16, 2004

No sign of Dimmick. I'm beginning to have my doubts about Wonder Valley. I thought it would be peaceful and restorative, but it's rather – distressing. The wind blows very hard, which is good for tumbleweeds but not so good for humans.

Made a grocery run down to Twenty-nine Palms. Passed a giant tumbleweed in a petrol station, so big it had lodged under the roof. By the time I turned around and came back, it was gone. "Monster tumbleweed," the attendant said. "Took off thataway." I headed up the dirt road he'd pointed to, but didn't find the tumbleweed. To tell the truth, I was a little afraid to find it. Had no idea they could get so big.

June 18, 2004

Still no Dimmick, so I finally drove out to the pub to look for him. I asked the bartender and he pointed to an old man in the corner booth with long white hair and a handlebar moustache. "Ask Teacher," he said.

Introduced myself to Teacher, who hadn't seen Dimmick, either. We shared a couple of beers and I discovered the old man had an MBA, a master's in electrical engineering, and some other master's he didn't stipulate. A couple more beers, and I learned he was one step away from earning all three degrees. "I have trouble with completion," he said. "A little like Bob Dimmick."

Christ, it's only been a week and I'm already beginning to feel like I'll never get out of this place. I've been in my share of remote locations, but never remember feeling this cut off – it's like another planet. A planet without water or contractors or art. Teacher did tell me about a field of tumbleweeds up near the Marine Base. I invited him to come and look at the garden when it was ready, and he said he'd try to schedule it in.

Schedule it into what?

Just as I was leaving, a group of Lady Marines came in and took over the pool table. That's what the bartender called them, "Lady Marines." One Lady Marine gave me the once-over. She looked like James Dean – clear-eyed, tan, with a shock of blond hair.

June 19, 2004
Bloody Dimmick. Bloody hell.

June 20, 2004
Have started collecting tumbleweeds anyway, keeping them in my rental Jeep. The spot Teacher directed me to was full of them. Golden tumbleweeds, blown up against an abandoned caravan, ripe for the picking. I had fifteen of them in the back when two soldiers turned up and asked me what I was doing. I said I was an artist doing a project for the Wonder Valley Arts Foundation and they seemed to find that amusing. One of them asked if I was from England. That met with his approval. "Tony Blair," he said. "He's a standup guy." Then he told me I better stay off military property if I didn't want to get caught up in a combat simulation. "Not everyone's trained to recognize an English accent," he said, and the other one nodded.

June 22, 2004
Dimmick, blessed Dimmick. Came in the afternoon and worked until three in the morning, putting up the two long sides of the fence. Worked like a maniac, with the strength of ten men. Didn't speak much, and wouldn't take water, despite the spittle collecting in the corners of his mouth. I did get him to take a photo. I'm sure he can finish tomorrow.

Dimmick constructing yellow plexiglas fence, taken by artist
Exterior of Wonder Valley Arts Foundation Artist's Residence, taken by artist
View of mountains, taken by artist
Artist dancing with plexiglas panel, taken by Dimmick

June 23, 2004
You guessed it. No Dimmick. Many unwanted visitors, though. The outside walls of the caravan are swarming with gnats and they're getting in somehow. They like to soak in my iced tea. Is it because of the heat? Christ, why is it so hot? Birds keep flying into the windows. They flop around on the ground, then flutter away, leaving ghostly wing prints on the glass.

Back from pub. Teacher was there, of course, but not Dimmick.

Teacher laughed. "Dimmick has a hard time keeping promises to a lady."

"I'm not a lady," I said. "I'm an artist."

When I got home I walked out to the garden under the full moon, which lights up the desert like a film set – so bright you can see your shadow. Three coyotes appeared at the open end of the fence and looked in at me. "Fuck off," I said, and they did.

Letter of Complaint

To the Wonder Valley Arts Foundation:

My husband was passing by your trailer today and spotted an English girl letting tumbleweeds out of her car. Naturally, he stopped and asked her what the hell she was doing. She said she wasn't letting them out, she was transferring them to the trailer for safekeeping. She said she was planning to make a tumbleweed garden.

We have let a lot of things pass out there at your so-called "artist's residence," but bringing tumbleweeds into the area is the last straw. Tumbleweeds bring down the property values. They make the area look uncared for. Boys use them for target practice. We didn't move up here to look at tumbleweeds. That yellow plastic fence she's putting up is ugly enough.

It's your land and this is a free country, but mark my words: if those tumbleweeds get loose, there'll be hell to pay.

Signed,

A Concerned Neighbor

Project Log

June 25, 2004

Two weeks and still no fourth wall. I've raked the dirt again and again but until Dimmick returns there's nothing else I can do. Drove down to the Barking Coyote tonight to drown my sorrows.

"Why's it called that?" I asked Teacher. "Don't coyotes howl?"

"They howl when they kill," he said. "They bark when they play."

He does know things. I asked him why he thinks people stop making, stop doing, stop everything.

"They get overwhelmed," he said. "They stop because they don't know where to start."

"Nothing wrong with stopping," he added, "so long as you resume. But you have to find a different way each time." He raised his glass and winked. "Like me – I stopped going to school and took up drinking."

There's something about the old man, though. I can see why they call him Teacher. He can't do anything for himself, and doesn't seem to do much for anyone else, but somehow he makes you want to. It's the way he looks at you, like he sees something there to believe in.

June 27, 2004

I've been spending way too much time at the Barking Coyote, but it's air-conditioned and serves unbelievably cheap beer – certainly an enterprise worth supporting?

Last night I slept in the room in back of the bar because I wasn't fit to drive. In the morning it smelled sickening, like stale hops. I stood up and gagged, then ran to the back door and threw it open. There was a jackrabbit standing less than ten feet away from me, its fur a silvery gray against the bright orange sky. Pretty! I cried, and puked. When I looked up again, it was gone.

June 30, 2004

Funny how fast things can turn around. First, James Dean came alone to the BC last night and bought me a drink. A couple of drinks. Then she gave me a ride on her motorbike, all the way down to the Salton Sea. Terrible, polluted place, an agricultural sump, basically, but a gorgeous sunrise over the water – electric pink. Shagged on a beach covered with fishbones.

When we got back to the residence, rosy with windburn and all else, GUESS WHO WAS THERE?

"Where you been?" Dimmick said crossly.

I shrugged and smiled. Like I owed him any explanation.

"Women," he said, shaking his head, and went to unload his truck.

July 1, 2004

Brilliant, I've got my fourth wall! And a hinged gate to get in and out of the garden. Today I let loose the tumbleweeds, but they didn't go far. There wasn't much wind and they mostly clumped together in the middle. Perhaps after being indoors for so long, they've forgotten how to tumble.

The nasty fellow who yelled at me about the garden the other day drove by, and he and his wife stopped the car and got out. The wife pointed to the tumbleweeds and shook her head. They both pretended not to see me. They looked around the outside of the fence for any stray tumbleweeds, then got back in the car and drove away.

My first critics.

July 3, 2004

The tumbleweeds are on the move. What a naff idea. Spent most of yesterday fighting the impulse to scrap the whole project. The solitary tumbleweed has more dignity somehow, rolling across the desert. When they're blowing around inside a fence like this, they look like a bunch of ne'er-do-wells.

July 4, 2004

Big party at the Barking Coyote for American Independence Day. Many jokes at my expense. Teacher introduced me to the editor of the Wonder Valley newpaper. She asked if she could interview me and I said sure. Nice old bat. Dotty hat – straw with giant paper roses.

Wonder Valley Gazette 7/5/04

ARTIST FINDS HERSELF IN TUMBLEWEED GARDEN
Rosalind Reed

Victoria Owens hails from London, and is currently an artist in residence at the Wonder Valley Arts Foundation. I met Victoria at the Barking Coyote, her favorite Wonder Valley haunt. "It's just like a pub at home!" she exclaimed, and from the looks of it, that's no amateur opinion.

RR: So what are you working on during your artist's residency, Victoria?

VO: An installation called Tumbleweed Garden. It's er – a garden made of tumbleweeds. Except they aren't stuck in the ground – they move about.

RR: And how's it coming?

VO: Well, I had a little trouble getting the fence up, but now it's in full swing.

RR: What does that mean, full swing?

VO: It means I've got loads of tumbleweeds blowing back and forth.

RR: And what does the actual gardening consist of?

VO: I go out every morning and separate the plants so they can keep rolling around. And then I rake the dirt.

RR: Tumbleweeds clump together, do they?

VO: Yes, that's what I've discovered. In an enclosed area, they become entangled.

RR: And what is the significance of Tumbleweed Garden?

VO (laughs, blushes): To be honest, in the beginning it was all a bit of a lark. But I've discovered that tumbleweeds have their own odd ways of being in the world, and that interests me. You'd think they would move however the wind is blowing, but the truth is you can never predict. It makes them rather captivating to watch.

RR: So your piece is about surprise?

VO: Yes, surprise and – eccentricity. Tumbleweeds are by definition eccentric.

RR: Now, would you describe what you're doing as land art?

VO: Sorry?

RR: Or as a "garden," does your project belong more to the realm of relational aesthetics?

VO: I – I'm sort of trying to get beyond the art world, really, those kinds of classifications.

RR: Oh, so you're an outsider artist now?

VO: Um, I don't think I could say that really, but I did feel the need for a change. . . the expectations were so... I felt... branded by my brand or something like that... (mumble mumble)... sorry, these are good questions, I just –

RR: Didn't think anyone would be asking them around here. I understand. Let's talk about something else then. How does it feel to be a Not-so-Young British Artist?

VO: Good God! Shall we get another drink? I'm not sure how to answer that question. I'm still fairly young, you know.

RR: Uh-huh. But I guess what I'm asking is, are you the real deal? Or is that what you've come here to find out?

VO: Oh, uh, I guess that's what I've come here to find out.

Project Log

July 6, 2004

Still recovering from my interview with that dreadful woman. Nice old bat my arse. Where did she come from? Why wasn't I warned? What does it mean to be "the real deal"? Who asks questions like that? It's as if I've landed on the set of some awful western.

The wind was up today and a tumbleweed came out of nowhere while I was raking and clapped me on the side of the head. Left two long, bleeding scratch marks on my neck. Bitch.

July 8, 2004

Killed a scorpion this morning in the kitchen near the sink. It was perfectly formed, just like the zodiac sign, with the segmented legs and tail. So perfectly formed, it cast a sort of spell over me. I stood there holding my shoe in the air, thinking, how can I possibly kill something so perfect and so deadly? I haven't got the will.

But I have, apparently, because I did.

July 10, 2004

Have suddenly started to paint again! Big empty canvases, nothing like what I used to do. Perhaps all those hours spent staring at the horizon waiting for Dimmick to appear have had their effect. What if I rented a little house out here after the residency and just painted all day? I could live on the light and the air – it's so good. Light and air and beer.

July 16, 2004

Haven't been to the bc for almost a week. Too busy. Dimmick came by today to see the garden. Made a show of checking the fence to make sure it holds. You can tell he's proud to be a part of the project, although the tumbleweeds disturbed him at first. He kept asking me, "Are you sure they're dead?" But after a while, he started to enjoy himself. "Look at that guy," he said. "He just keeps on rolling."

Dimmick genders the tumbleweeds according to their motility. The ones that stick to the fence are female. The ones that bounce around are male.

PHOTOS:
"Male" tumbleweeds, taken by artist
"Female" tumbleweeds, taken by artist

July 22, 2004
Knocked off early today and drove down to the BC. Ran into that Reed woman again – she's not so bad "off the record." We had a drink and I asked her how she knows so much about art. Turns out she's an artist, too – she came for a Wonder Valley Arts Foundation residency back in the seventies and never left. Wouldn't talk about her work, though. There was no electricity back then, is all she said. You had to use candles.

At sunset she came up to see the garden, and watched the tumbleweeds blow around for a long time without saying anything. The sky was purple and gold, like a beautiful bruise, when I finally asked her what she thought. No answer. I looked over and saw that she was crying.

"You did it," she said in a strange little voice. "You really did it."

The roses on her silly hat were trembling.

July 24, 2004
James Dean turned up again today. Says she's getting ready to ship out. I found out she's a helicopter pilot.

"Why didn't you tell me that before?" I asked.

"Why would I?" she said. "Do you know a lot about helicopters?"

"Sorry," she said, as we were walking out to the garden. "I just like to keep the different parts of my life separate. I have to. By the way, you're not using my real name in that log, are you?"

She didn't get to see the garden in action. It was a very windy day and by the time we got out there, in the late afternoon, the tumbleweeds were all tangled up into two big masses. They sat facing each other, intransigent. It's going to be hell separating them out.

PHOTOS:
Tumbleweed mass 1, taken by artist
Tumbleweed mass 2, taken by artist

July 25, 2004
James Dean stayed over and we made a bonfire out of the tumbleweeds. They were too far gone – I'll have to get new ones tomorrow.

"Too bad," she said, lighting a cigarette and flicking the match on to the pyre. "I would've liked to see them blowing around."

I told her I was afraid to go back to London, I've found such peace here in the desert. Peace and anonymity.

"Nobody's anonymous in the desert," she said. "People can see you coming from miles away."

"Did you see me coming?"

James Dean exhaled deeply. "Did I ever."

July 26, 2004
Never thought I'd have a thing for a soldier. But an Army helicopter passed over yesterday while I was out collecting tumbleweeds and I jumped up and down and waved my arms like a mad woman. "James Dean! James Dean!" I yelled, only I used her real name.

Twenty or thirty people from town dropped by this afternoon to take a look at the garden, which is full of tumbleweeds again. I get more visitors every day. A German photographer stopped by too and took some photos, which made me nervous. Not sure I'm ready for the work to leave Wonder Valley.

July 30, 2004
Teacher finally came to see the garden today, and not a minute too soon. My residency ends tomorrow. "Fast little buggers," is

all he said, but he stayed for a while. I told him I'd rented a place nearby, with a Quonset hut out back for a studio. I didn't tell him about James Dean.

Teacher shook his head. "Go back to England," he said. "You did what you came to do. Don't get stuck here like the rest of us."

"You're not stuck," I said. "You're one step away from three degrees."

"Exactly," he said.

"What was the third master's going to be?"

Teacher bowed stiffly into the hot dry wind. "Fine Arts."

"You've got to be joking!"

He shook his head.

"I'd like to ask you some questions about that," I said, "but right now I've got to get these tumbleweeds back into the Jeep."

"What for?"

"I'm going to set them free out near the base. I would turn them loose right here, but I'm afraid of what the neighbors might do."

"Go ahead and let them out," Teacher said. "Back in the day, this area was full of tumbleweeds."

"And the neighbors?"

He shrugged. "They don't own Wonder Valley."

And with that, Teacher and I walked around the garden together one last time, took some more photos and opened the gate.

PHOTOS:
Tumbleweed Garden, north side, taken by artist
Tumbleweed Garden, east side, taken by artist
Tumbleweed Garden, south side, taken by artist
Tumbleweed Garden, west side, taken by artist
Artist shepherding tumbleweeds to freedom, taken by Teacher
Solitary tumbleweed rolling across desert, taken by the artist

7
BUNKER MENTALITY

She lucked out, that's all. They say the laziest man is also the most efficient, and in her case this was not just a truism but true. Because she was one of those people who never prepare for anything, not tornadoes or hurricanes or blackouts or Christmas. She was one of those people who every once in a while started to wonder why she or anybody had to work. *You work to pay the rent,* a voice would come to her from far away, and that would settle it, until she started to wonder why you had to pay the rent and so on, until eventually the voice sighed and went away. In short, she wasn't the kind of person who would build a bunker.

How did she end up in someone else's bunker? Well, when she wasn't talking to the voice, she liked to listen to the radio, and one day the radio said that a terrorist cell had taken control of a batch of Russian nuclear missiles and trained them on the United States. She didn't hear the rest of the report because she was reminded of the bunker at the end of her street her neighbors had been working on since before y2k, and she decided to wander down and check it out. She was interested in other people's preparations, even if – or perhaps especially because – she never made any of her own.

Of course, she didn't think the missiles were going to go off right then – nobody did – but she was down in the bunker looking around when the sirens started up, those whiny old air raid sirens from wwii. Usually they stopped after five minutes or so, but this time they kept going, so she decided to close the thick steel door just to be safe. Then she sat and waited for the old man and his sons to come. She would've opened up for them – it was their bunker, after all – or so she told herself, but she never had to stand the test because nobody came, then, or ever.

Sometimes she had to pinch herself to make sure it was all real. Because who would've thought? Who would've thought fourteen-foot concrete walls could actually withstand blast and heat and radioactive fallout? Who would've thought her neighbors could really stockpile a year's worth of food and water? Who would've thought the generator and the cistern and the weird toilet arrangement they'd dreamed up would actually work?

She felt sorry for the people who'd prepared for the other catastrophe, the biochemical attack, the ones who'd stored away flashlights and three days' worth of food and water and lined the baby's room with plastic sheeting. Preparing for the wrong disaster is worse than not preparing at all.

But the last president, the Cowboy President, had convinced them it was a whole new world they were living in, a World of Terror. In this new world, everybody had to go it alone, especially Americans, and the only language anyone understood anymore was the language of force and intimidation. As if the old world hadn't been a world of terror, too. As if the world hadn't always been terrible and terrifying but somehow people had managed to keep their chins up and be decent to each other and even found a republic or two.

If it had been her caught out like that, having readied for the wrong disaster, she would've gone up on the roof to watch the missiles land, like they used to do with the A-bomb tests at Vegas casinos. Stay up all night drinking and catch one really good last show. Turn to the others and say, when your number's up your number's up. This was not just a truism now, but true.

Oh, did she feel bad for humankind. Ashamed, too. She knew she would feel that shame her whole life, even if her life only lasted a few more years. You know how something can be bothering you without your really being aware of it, a mistake or a problem looming over you like a shadow, but when you turn and face it head on, it turns out not to be as bad as you thought? Well, this was nothing like that.

At some point she found a photo album in a trunk. It must've belonged to the older son because there were lots of pictures of him with his wife and baby. She hadn't known her neighbors except to say hi, so looking through their album felt a little weird, but what else was there for her to do? When she moved in they were all living together in the house at the end of the street, a falling down place with a double lot – the old man, his two sons, his older son's wife and the baby. She'd heard about it when the older son got divorced, though, heard about it because he and his wife had a screaming fight and all of the windows were open.

You could tell from the photos that all was not right. There was one picture of him – he had long stringy blond hair – looking down at the baby, who had short stringy blond hair – a look both proud and distrustful, as if he knew she looked like him and wasn't sure he wanted to know any more people who looked like him. Ambivalent, you could call it. The baby herself was anything but ambivalent – she was smiling and waving a spoon in the air. Somebody had dressed her in a furry pink thing, but it didn't appear to be cramping her style. She was what babies should be: upbeat. Her mom, on the other hand, looked tired and shifty-eyed, like she was having an affair or was about to have one or was thinking to herself that she ought to have one.

It was funny to look at that photo and know that those people had been once and weren't any longer. Funny in a stomach-turning kind of way. There was another photo toward the end, after the wife and the baby had disappeared, of the older son with his father and brother. The old man looked like a lunatic, she'd always thought that about him when she passed him on the street. With his long gray beard and beady black eyes, he was obviously the man behind the bunker, the man who'd capitalized on his older son's distress and loneliness. "Forget that bitch and come round back," she could hear him saying. "We've got shit to do."

The younger son she'd always kind of liked. He smiled whenever he saw her, a joyful, loving smile that took her breath away. "Don't mind him, he's autistic," the old man told her once gruffly. "He's not smiling at you, he's thinking about something else." The younger son had that same smile in the photo, which looked like it was taken in the bunker. She wondered what the something else was that the younger son was always thinking about, the thing that made him smile, and felt sad because now she would never know. Then she realized she never would've known anyway, and that made her feel better.

She found some country music CDs in the trunk too and put them on. Listening to country music seemed like as good a way as any of getting through a nuclear winter. Her favorite song was "Mamas Don't Let Your Babies Grow Up to Be Cowboys," by Willie Nelson. She especially liked the way Willie changed the refrain at the end to "Mamas Don't Let Your Cowboys Grow Up to be Babies." Because it was Cowboy Babies that had gotten them into this mess, but Willie could make you chuckle about that, or at least shake your head and sigh, instead of moaning and rocking back and forth, or sitting frozen for hours, thinking about the world that had blown away like snow.

Her thinking about the world took certain paths, since it's a big thing to think about all at once. For starters, she thought about bridges and vaulted arches. Then she thought about sidewalks and carpets, and how once people had cared where they put their feet and had had feet to put there. She thought about mathematics and physics and natural science, too – in a general way, because she'd never understood them, although she'd always known they were there. She thought about paintings – again, not specific paintings, because she didn't know much about art, but the mere fact of paintings. She thought about shoes. She thought about coats and watches and spectacles. She thought about tea kettles and space heaters and mandolines. She thought about books. She thought about books a lot because she liked to read. She thought about bookshelves and couches and chairs, and other kinds of furniture, such as ottomans. She thought about suitcases, especially the ones on wheels. She thought about sports, which were supposed to replace war, but didn't. She thought about newspapers. She thought about businesses, like restaurants and dry cleaners and pet stores. She thought about houses, all through the ages. All through the ages there had been houses, and now there were only bunkers.

She thought about coffins and tombstones. She thought about bottles and cans. She thought about brooms, buckets and vacuum cleaners. She thought about boats and ships. She thought about all of the great inventions she'd learned about in junior high: the steam engine and the airplane and the cotton gin. She still thought the best one was the traffic light, which was invented by a black man, who also invented the gas mask. Three colors, three commands, and nobody gets hurt. So much better than the multi-colored terrorism alert system. She thought about escalators and elevators. She thought about telephones, and the Internet. Couldn't the Internet have stopped this from happening? She thought about drugs and alcohol, and wished that she had some.

She thought about the rest of the world, but being an American, she didn't have a very clear picture of it. She thought about all of those different societies with their different histories and textiles. Different kinds of music, and ways of treating the mentally ill. Oh yeah, and different languages. And she thought about all of the people who'd fought to be free – not just in the American way, in their own way. That was as far as she could go with that.

She also thought about animals. She thought about them all the time. On one level it was okay that there were no more humans or human inventions – after all, humans were also responsible for things like toxic waste and television and, of course, nuclear missiles. But that there should be no more dogs? Or horses? Or cheetahs? That there should be no more coyotes or hawks or lizards? No more elephants? No more lions? No more dolphins? No more pigs? No more piglets? No more lambs? A world without chickens? A world without fish? A world without cows? A world without robins, sparrows or pigeons? A world without trees?

But sometimes she forgot about it all for days at a time. Or maybe they were just nights. Stretches, she forgot about it for stretches. During those stretches, she continued to make her way through her neighbors' CD collection, which was mostly country, and their books, which were mostly ham radio manuals and biographies of business tycoons. There was a book on metalcrafts, too. Metalcrafts are things like horseshoe wine racks and tin can soap dishes.

She thought the bunker showed a much better use of their time and energy. It was (apparently) soundly built, with an open plan – one big room with a galley kitchen and a bathroom off to one side. They hadn't gotten around to painting the concrete walls or carpeting the floors, but that made it more spacious – chic even, in a lofty kind of way, if you overlooked the fact that there were no windows.

The illusion was further compromised by the three plaid La-z-Boy recliners in one corner, but she didn't mind. They were extremely comfortable. She did feel a little guilty for lying around in her neighbors' chairs when they'd obviously been such hard workers. Anything but lazy boys. It was like Goldilocks and the Three Bears, except without the Three Bears.

Or Goldilocks. She couldn't remember the last time she'd washed her hair. Bathing was hard, psychologically. At first it made you forget about everything, that elemental contact with water, but then it made you remember. It made you remember something you couldn't possibly remember, which was being bathed in the kitchen sink as a baby. And that made you think, why didn't I just drown?

But if she fell asleep without remembering, she'd wake up crying. Gasping, to be more precise, and clawing at the air. To avoid this, before she went to bed in those stretches she called night, she would repeat to herself three times: the world is gone and you are all alone, the world is gone and you are all alone, the world is gone and you are all alone. Then she'd weep quietly until she nodded off to sleep – for the monkeys and the oceans and all of the people she would never see again. Of course, she wept for her mother and father, who'd bathed her in the kitchen sink, but she wept for other people, too, sometimes people she'd only seen in passing, who'd looked like they might be nice.

It wasn't all weeping, though. There were days when she actually felt happy. Like the day she realized there were no more celebrities. Or reality TV shows. Or hidden cameras. Or dating services. No more malls. No more tract housing. No more oil companies, drug companies or timber companies. No more discounts.

There was the day she realized she would never have to learn how to care for her coffee beans. Not only that, but she could eat out of cans for the rest of her life. She had never thrown a dinner party, and now she would never have to.

Now she would never have to get a real job. She would never have to prepare a resume. She would never have to live up to her parents' expectations. She would never again wander out of the supermarket without paying and have to go back and face the checker.

She wouldn't have to wonder anymore why she formed unhealthy attachments, when she formed attachments at all. She wouldn't have to stand at the window in the middle of the night next to a sleeping stranger, watching the cars go back and forth on the highway. She could stop working on herself, working on relationships, working period. How great was that?

But one day or stretch, the voice started to give her a hard time.

You can either lie around here until you die, the voice said, *or you can figure out how to use that ham radio over in the corner and find out what's happened.*

"I want to go outside," she answered.

Hey, the voice said firmly. *That is not an option.*

So she taught herself ham radio, as best she could from the manual. She got as far as understanding how to listen in, to tune into the frequency and all of that, but she couldn't figure out how to transmit. She thought there might be a piece of equipment missing.

Still she sat in front of the receiver, listening to crackles and pops. She did this every day for a long time, in between breakfast and dinner. She ate lunch at her desk. To tell the truth, it was the closest she'd ever come to real work. When she was a temp, back when there were offices, she used to take two and three hour lunches. Sometimes she wouldn't go back to the office at all. Nobody ever seemed to notice, whereas if she stuck around, she invariably broke the copier and everybody noticed. They would tell her it wasn't her fault and then they would ask the agency to send somebody out to replace her.

But this was different. This work was meaningful. She was searching for life in the void. She recorded all of her findings, which were zero, in a little yellow notebook.

The yellow notebook was almost full before she heard anybody speak. It was a man's voice, and it said, "Is anybody there?" She waited for a long time, but nobody answered. That night or stretch she wept long and hard before going to sleep. She wept because now she knew someone else had survived the end of the world. In some ways, that was worse than bearing it alone.

Soon she started to hear place names. She'd read in one of the manuals that this is what ham radio operators spend a lot of their time doing—identifying where they are. Once she heard somebody say "Yucca Valley, California." Another time she heard "Chico, California." Then it was "Waimea, Hawaii." "Carpinteria, California." "Hilo, Hawaii." She started to wonder if anyone had survived outside of small towns in California and Hawaii. Once she heard a woman say New York, but it was more of a question than a statement. "New York?"

There were never any two-way conversations. It was as if only she could hear them all. Sometimes she thought that was a terrible thing, and sometimes she thought it was just fine. Maybe everyone needed a little time away from each other before things started up again.

She had a strange dream one night or stretch (it could've been a vision), after eating a particularly brightly colored meal (her neighbors were big fans of processed cheese). In her dream or vision that night or stretch, she'd left the bunker and was heading for Hawaifornia in an old Model T Ford. Just to explain Hawaifornia: In her dream world the only two states in America to be missed by missiles (after the u.s. fired back at the terrorists, and Russia retaliated) were Hawaii and California, which had now formed their own union. This was made easier by the fact that Hawaii had floated a lot closer to California, until they were almost touching. People went back and forth between the two states in glass-bottomed tourist boats with the glass covered over. Nobody wanted to see what was in the water.

On the way out to Hawaifornia, black dust swirled all around her Model T, blotting out the sun. Every now and then she pulled the car over and got out to inspect a piece of straw that had been drilled through a tree trunk by the blast. That's when she knew it was a dream, because that was in the film about hurricanes she'd seen in ninth-grade civics class.

When she got to Oklahoma, she started to see other Model T Fords heading in the same direction. The drivers all wore bandanas over their mouths to keep out the dust. But there was something else in the air besides dust, something heavy that burned her lips and eyeballs. She figured this was radiation.

Oklahoma must've been a lot closer to California than it used to be, too, because she made it there in no time. Literally no time, because it was a dream. When she got to Hawaifornia, the dust and the heaviness disappeared, which is how she knew she'd arrived. That, and the fields of orange poppies and the leis people strung around her neck at intersections. They all seemed to be musicians, those people, there was music everywhere, and homemade preserves and bags of pecans and crocheted slippers continually changing hands. When she asked someone about it, a woman with her mother's face, the woman smiled and said, this is what we do all day long now. It's a new new world.

And then, because somehow in the new new world she was somebody very very important, she asked them to take her to their leader, the Governor of Hawaifornia, and they did. To her delight, he turned out not to be Arnold Schwarzenegger but Willie Nelson. That made sense, in a way, because Willie Nelson has taken part in more collaborations than any other solo artist in recording history.

"What are you planning for this new new world, Willie?" she said, slapping him on the back. In her dream or vision it was like they were old friends.

"We're going to build a bridge between Hawaii and California," Willie said, taking the red, white and blue bandana off his mouth and wrapping it around his head. "And make a lot of music."

Walking with Willie towards the spot where the bridge was going to be, she saw a beautiful pink cloud shimmering on the horizon.

"That's Hawaii," he said, in his twangy voice. It sounded like the beginning of a song.

"Boy, is this great," she said. "What a world, huh Willie? What a world!"

Willie nodded and tossed his long red braids over his shoulder with a joyful, loving smile. He strummed a few chords on his old guitar, which sounded better than ever.

But just then they heard a terrible ruckus, a howling and a whooping with some gurgles thrown in.

"What's that noise?" she cried. "That's not music!"

Willie pointed to a field nearby, where a bunch of babies were riding horses and waving guns.

"Oh no! Not them again."

"Yep." Willie shook his head and sucked his teeth. "Cowboy Babies."

When she woke up back down in the bunker, she was weeping. First, because she wasn't all the way awake, she wept for the fact that there were still Cowboy Babies in the world, even after all that had happened, and because she missed Willie Nelson. Then she wept because she would never see her mother's face, or a woman with her mother's face, again.

She wept because sometime soon she would finish all of the food and water and have to leave the bunker. Then she would get sick and die. She wept because there was no way, absolutely no way, around this. She wept because she didn't want it to end.

She wept because she thought she was starting to go a little crazy. She could've sworn she'd heard a car start, and the sound of a barking dog. Once she even thought she heard a man say, "Who shut the goddamn door?"

When people use the expression "bunker mentality," they're trying to say you've turned your back on the world. They're trying to say you think everybody's out to get you. And it's true, this was the mentality that had built the bunker, and this was the mentality that had caused the series of events that put her, an unprepared sort of person, down there. But once you're actually in the bunker, your state of mind is completely different. You want nothing more than to get out. You want nothing more than to face the world, and give it one more chance. That is the one thing you want, and that is the one thing you can't have.

Once you've accepted the situation, though, you can live in a bunker for a very long time – or at least until your food and water runs out. Your mind may play tricks on you, but that's all it is. Humans are wired to need other humans, which may be part of the problem. Other humans take advantage of that sometimes.

She thought about writing a manual about living in a bunker, now that she'd been doing it for some time, but then she realized that everybody who would ever need it was already living in a bunker. So instead, and to drown out the shouts and the pounding on the door by the men she knew were not there, she put on a little country music and lowered her recliner.

8

WHEN I RETIRE

The blue desert sky was stippled with tiny white clouds the day Adelaide drove Don and Hazel out to Twentynine Palms to see about the Vietnam Vet and his girlfriend. A long black ribbon of highway stretched out before them, seemingly without end or other occupants, and the mood in the car was solemn. Being retired is not all fun and games.

Not that Adelaide was retired, mind you. Not officially, anyway. She was still a fairly young woman, but she'd recently ended a long relationship and bought a little weekend house in the desert, so she felt retired, or at least semi-retired. She also felt tired. Her long relationship had been with an attorney, and she was worn out from arguing.

Attorneys, she'd discovered, do not take kindly to ambivalence, especially towards the future. If you cannot make a firm statement, an Attorney will make one for you. No sitting on the fence. This used to bother Adelaide a lot, but nowadays when she was sitting on the fence, watching the quail bobble around her yard at sunset, she had a feeling of great calm. The calm that comes when you've given up the fight.

The only downside was that, without the fight, Adelaide didn't know what to do with herself. She slept a lot and went for walks and ended up spending a lot of time next door with her neighbors, Don and Hazel. Don and Hazel were legitimately retired, and Adelaide felt glad of it every time she sank into the bottomless sofa in the neat front parlor of their doublewide. Glad to be with others who had given up the fight.

Don and Hazel had an ancient pug named Buster who hadn't

quite given up the fight, although he was going paralyzed in his back legs. When Buster wasn't going paralyzed in his back legs, he was going around in circles with an equilibrium problem. When he wasn't going around in circles with an equilibrium problem, he was standing on the back of the sofa, breathing down on Adelaide with a terrible foul breath.

They could while away the entire afternoon, Adelaide, Don, Hazel and Buster, talking about different things. Well, mostly it was Hazel talking, and mostly it was Hazel talking about death – not her own so much as other people's – but that was okay, because she told good stories. Her stories fell mainly into three categories: death by brown recluse spider bite, death by tumor, and death by drunk driver going down the wrong side of the highway.

Some of these things had happened to members of Hazel and Don's own family, and as she was telling the stories Hazel would point to the relevant family member in the large eighties-era photograph-cum-oil painting on the wall. The girls all looked like Don with feathered hair, and the boys all looked like Hazel with a mullet. "The middle daughter's sister-in-law," Hazel would say, pointing. "The son-in-law's father." And most sadly, in the case of the brown recluse spider bite, "The eldest son."

But Hazel's best story wasn't a death story at all. It was a story of survival. It was about the time the motor home caught on fire. "Get ready to bail, Mother," Don said when he saw the heat gauge rising. "We're about to blow."

Whenever Adelaide told a story of her own, Hazel sat like an owl with a careful, surprised look on her face, thinking up a better one. If Adelaide's drunk driver had killed a newlywed couple, Hazel's drunk driver had killed a newborn coming home from the hospital. If Adelaide's tumor was the size of a grapefruit, Hazel's was the size of a cantaloupe. You get the picture.

Don talked about death a lot, too, but mostly his own. He was resigned to it. Almost cheerful.

"Didn't think I would last this long," he liked to say.

Don had been in the Navy and his arms and chest were covered with blurry tattoos. Whenever Adelaide came over for a visit, he struggled out of his La-z-Boy and smiled shyly as she hugged him. Then he went into the bedroom and put a t-shirt on.

After Don got out of the Navy he became a metal worker, and Hazel kept the books in the cooling business that employed him. Later on they started their own business. Now Don did crafts on days when his back wasn't bothering him too much, and Hazel crocheted slippers, five or six pairs a week. When Adelaide first moved in, Don and Hazel brought her over a pair of pink and orange slippers and a Formica cheese board in the shape of a pig. Next it was a pair of pink and purple slippers and a cactus sculpture made out of horseshoes. After that Don made her a roadrunner weathervane and installed it in her front yard, right in the spot where the sun went down. That meant there was always a roadrunner in her sunset, but that was okay.

One day Adelaide was trying to think what she could make for Don and Hazel in return – what craft she might take up, because right now she had none – when she remembered she was not actually retired. She still had a job teaching fourth grade in L.A. Nevertheless, she felt shiftless compared to Don and Hazel.

The Attorney had thought she was shiftless too. Shiftless or – when he was being generous – depressed. And it was true, she did lie around a lot. But her grandmother had done that, too. Before she met Don and Hazel and saw how industrious they were, Adelaide used to think maybe she was just precocious. She had an old lady name. Maybe her parents had sensed something.

The truth is, Adelaide had wanted to be an old lady for as long as she could remember – or no, to be a young lady who lived like an old lady. Except for the aches and pains, she reasoned, old people had it pretty good. They weren't expected to have babies or cocktail parties or even wear clothes that fit right. They weren't expected to remember other people's names, or always be up on the news. They didn't have to attend law firm retreats or parent-teacher conferences or couples counseling. They didn't have to be in the same place at the same time every day, and stay in that place for hours. Although many of them did that, they didn't have to. And when old people talked about death like it was right there, staring them in the face, nobody told them to cut it out.

When she was a kid, Adelaide spent summer weekdays at her grandmother's apartment while her parents were working. She and her grandmother lay around talking all day and never got bored. When it cooled off in the late afternoon, her grandmother would throw on a muumuu and have her friends over to play cards on the balcony and drink whiskey sours. Adelaide felt at home with those terse old men in the battered fedoras and their gushy old lady-friends with the false eyelashes. "Girlie," they'd say, as she refilled their glasses. "You're one of us."

When Adelaide shared these fond memories with the Attorney, and confessed that retirement was the only future she had ever imagined for herself, she thought he would laugh and say, "Me too!" Instead he scowled and said that retirement was not a future. Retirement was the absence of a future, and they had their whole lives ahead of them. He, for one, was planning to have a brilliant career. Plus, according to the Attorney, they had to earn their retirement.

Adelaide considered that a copout. "Retirements aren't given," she pointed out. "Retirements are taken."

The Attorney was not convinced. What would they do after they retired?

"We'll play bocci ball and go to Catalina on the ferry."

How would they live?

"Like retirees."

Which isn't to say Adelaide didn't have her own doubts. She would feel bad abandoning her nine year-olds to the rat race, but they needed a teacher with a different agenda anyway. One who would try to prepare them for life's triumphs and adversities – somebody who cared about all that. A teacher who didn't hog the tire swing at recess, thumbing through the AARP bulletin.

Although Adelaide's class had a reputation for good behavior, it wasn't through any labor of hers. Her students just couldn't seem to be bothered with fighting or name-calling. At recess, they sat around playing checkers and reading the newspaper, their faces turned toward the sun.

But even Adelaide's students had to draw the line somewhere.

This became clear on Career Day, when – after the invited guests (an attorney, a doctor, a florist, and an undertaker) had all departed – Adelaide took a few minutes to tell them about one more option they might want to consider.

"Retirement is not a career," protested an apple-cheeked boy named Arthur.

"Really, Arthur?" Adelaide said icily. Apple-cheeked boys rubbed her the wrong way. They looked so fresh.

"What is retirement?" another student asked.

"It's like having recess," Adelaide said quickly. "All of the time."

"Retirement is what you do when you get old," Arthur piped up again. "If you retire before you get old, it's called welfare and it's not fair to people who have to work."

"Now that's an interesting point of view," Adelaide said, rolling her eyes at the other children. "Tell us, Arthur, what do you want to be when you grow up?"

Arthur folded his little arms. "An attorney."

Arthur, Arthur, she wanted to say. Why not skip over all of that? Paint a band of red or light blue over that part of your life. The intrigues and the betrayals, the promotions and the setbacks, the wives and/or the boyfriends, the kids, the houses, the insurance policies – it's all of a piece, Arthur. And it's not the piece that matters.

Instead she said, "Good for you, Arthur, good for you," because it probably was good for him.

After Career Day, some of the parents complained to the school that Adelaide had been suggesting unnatural things to the children. The principal was relieved to hear her side of the story.

"It's never too early to start planning your retirement," he said.

"It never is," Adelaide agreed.

Adelaide stopped for gas in Twentynine Palms and Don and Hazel went to use the toilets. Their property was to the north of town, still a twenty-minute ride. An armored car rattled by as Adelaide was filling up her tank, then another, then another, on their way up to the Marine Base. Back from Iraq? she wondered idly, watching them disappear into the sun-blasted horizon.

Adelaide had been on one other outing with her neighbors a few months before – a pleasure excursion to Giant Rock, a locale that featured prominently in Don and Hazel's conversation. Back in the fifties it had been the spot for extraterrestrial sightings in their parts and they'd spent a lot of time out there with their kids.

"Did you ever see anything?" Adelaide asked.

"Oh sure," Don said. "Back then? Back then the skies were full of UFOS. Back then it felt like any day now!"

"Any day now what?"

Don looked over at Hazel.

"Any day now we'd be, you know, contacted," she replied.

The two of them talked about Giant Rock with such fondness that one day, on a whim, Adelaide had offered to drive them out there. She was curious herself, although had she known how long it was going to take, she might've thought twice. She was just beginning to wonder what would happen to the three of them if her dinged-up old Honda conked out on the sandy access road, when they rounded a corner and ran right into it.

She screeched to a halt and Don whistled. "Would you look at that?"

The rock, which was freestanding, had been spray painted all over with racial slurs and heart equations, a stony testament to human weakness. More interestingly, at least for the moment, there was a man lying on top of it pointing a rifle at them.

"Jesus!" Adelaide slammed the car into reverse and didn't stop until they hit the blacktop.

"Who was that guy?" she gasped, pressing her forehead to the steering wheel. "What did he want?"

"You never can tell with people," Hazel said, with a little laugh. She was clearly jazzed by the encounter – Adelaide could see her filing it away with the burning motor home under near-death experiences – but Don shook his head sorrowfully.

"No wonder the aliens don't come around any more."

Don didn't believe in violence, not anymore. Hazel had to tell his war stories for him. At Okinawa, she told Adelaide, he'd had to sail right past men who were drowning and calling out for help.

"Sail right past!" she said proudly. "That was the order."

Also at Okinawa, Don's buddy Tony's arm got blown off during a Kamikaze attack and ended up on his buddy Fred's chest.

"So Fred starts yelling 'Get it off! Get it off me!' and Don picks it up and puts it back down next to Tony, and Tony yells, 'Whose goddamn arm is that?'"

While Hazel talked, Don stared straight ahead with his hands on his knees, his bullfrog eyes filled with tears. Only once did he interrupt to say, "We figured out how to make all those fancy bombs but we still don't know how to make World Peace."

Don didn't believe in violence anymore, but he did believe in the Military. He felt the Military had been very good to him, even though as a result of a back injury he sustained in the service he'd been in crippling pain for the last thirty years. Even though the VA sent him the wrong medicine every other time.

"The Military takes care of their people," he said.

Hazel liked the Military, too, but she wasn't so keen on World Peace, especially if it was going to be handed down by the New World Order. She had a sign up over her washing machine that said GET US OUT, and then in smaller print, OF THE UNITED NATIONS.

"Everybody should just do for themselves," she liked to say.

Adelaide had a feeling she and Hazel might not have been friends if Hazel hadn't been retired, but since she was, they were, and there was lots she and Adelaide and Don could talk about without running into trouble. Birds, for instance – although Adelaide and Don tended to talk about baby quails hatching, and Hazel tended to talk about owls swooping down at twilight and tearing out the throats of little dogs. Lately she'd grown preoccupied with all of the snake mixing that was going on in their area – cross-breeding between poisonous Mojave greens and harmless pink-tailed racers. The offspring, she was fond of pointing out, were all poisonous.

Sometimes Adelaide thought Hazel had to be so bored by Don, but at other times she could see why she loved him. He was so okay with his own softness, he made it okay for her to be soft, too.

The Attorney could've taken a lesson from Hazel. Hell, Adelaide could've taken a lesson from Don.

She was trying to take a lesson now. Every evening, as she was sitting on her fence watching the sun go down, Don walked out with Buster to shut the gate. She wasn't sure either one of them saw her, because their eyesight wasn't so good anymore, but if they did, they pretended that they didn't, and she didn't call out, content to watch them trundle along, man and dog, their gaits somehow perfectly matched, perhaps because they were both going paralyzed in their back legs. It was a study in softness: Don and Buster trundling and the owls hoo-hooting and the purple mountains melting into the charcoal sky.

Adelaide paid for the gas and she and Hazel and Don got back in the car and proceeded north on the road the armored cars had taken. As they approached the Marine base, the land emptied out until there were no houses or Joshua trees at all, nothing to break up the immense wide flatness – so flat it looked a little bit curved. A few mountains in the distance, maybe, but not big ones.

Don directed Adelaide onto a washboard road, the road to the property. When Hazel inherited the forty acre lot from her brother the year before, friends of his – a Vietnam vet and his girlfriend – were already living there in a trailer, so Hazel and Don had let them stay on. But recently the Vet had chased off two of their grandsons who'd gone up there to camp, plus he'd changed the combination lock on the gate going in. Two of the forty acres were enclosed in a sturdy chain link fence, which is something people do with their property in the desert just to show that they're around. Chain link fences and KEEP OUT signs.

Hazel and Don had asked their one remaining son to drive out there with them so they could see what was going on, but he hadn't been able to make the time. And so Adelaide had offered to take them – against her better judgment, after what happened at Giant Rock – and now here they were, the three of them, bumping down the road on their way to meet another potential killer.

As they approached the fence, Don directed her to pull up next to the gate. The Vet's trailer, a rusty little Airstream, was in the corner of the fenced-in area nearest them, surrounded by two junked cars, a refrigerator without a door, a broken TV and a purple lawn chair.

"Look at that mess!" Don said, shaking his head. "Beep your horn."

She did, but nobody came out.

"The bag, Mother," Don said. Hazel handed him a gym bag Adelaide hadn't noticed before. "You ladies wait here," he said.

Hazel got out anyway, but Adelaide obeyed Don's directive, telling herself she should be ready with the getaway car in case anything went wrong. That was her way of pretending not to be chicken. For a long time, Don and Hazel fussed around with the lock on the gate and nothing happened. Gun noises drifted down from the base like distant thunder and the tiny clouds tucked up under each other, forming a band of white across the bright blue sky. A battered old jackrabbit hopped around a creosote bush on snowshoe feet. What peace! Adelaide thought. What peace I've found.

When she looked back dreamily toward the gate, Don was bashing the lock open with a hammer. She scrambled out of her car and the Vet burst out of his trailer at the exact same moment.

"Hey!" the Vet yelled.

"What are you doing?" Adelaide shrieked.

Don swung open the gate and trundled in the direction of the trailer.

"Don't worry, honey," Hazel greeted Adelaide. "I've got him covered."

"What is that?"

"Snakecharmer ii," Hazel said, leveling a pellet gun at the Vet. "I keep it for killing snakes."

"But Don doesn't believe in violence!"

"This isn't violence," Hazel said, shifting the gun higher on her shoulder. "This is deterrence."

Adelaide gave up on Hazel and hurried to catch up with Don, hoping she could convince the Vet he was having some kind of episode and lead him quietly back to the car. But when she got to where they were standing, the Vet was the one apologizing.

"Damn," he said, hanging his head. He had that angry red tan guys get from passing out drunk in the sun. "I didn't know they were your grandkids."

"I raised two boys to men," Don said. "I know what acting out looks like."

"Yes, sir," the Vet said, straightening up. He was tall and narrow-shouldered, in his mid-fifties, maybe, with a dyed red pompadour. He reminded Adelaide of a Roman candle.

"Girlfriend left you, huh?" Don said.

The Vet nodded and looked over at Adelaide shyly.

"She's not interested in you," Don said. "She's a teacher."

The Vet hung his head again.

"You promise to clean up around here," Don said, "we'll let you stay. But no more fooling with the lock."

The Vet nodded and waved sheepishly at Hazel. Hazel lowered Snakecharmer II and waved back.

In the car on the way home Hazel fell asleep, worn out from all the excitement. Adelaide took the opportunity to have a few words with Don.

"It might've been better just to kick him off the property and get it over with – I mean, while you were out there armed and ready, so to speak. He seems like a nice guy, but very unstable."

Don looked at her like she was crazy. "Where's he going to go?"

"That's not your concern. He'll find a way to make things work."

"If he hasn't found a way already," Don said, looking out the window, "I seriously doubt that would do it."

Adelaide was silent the rest of the way, adjusting her thinking. She could see now that she'd been wrong, Don and Hazel hadn't given up the fight. Perhaps Don and Hazel had only just begun to fight.

People always say, when I retire, I'm going to golf every day, or, when I retire, I'm going to travel. When I retire, I'm going to read the paper in my pajamas, like I do on Sunday mornings. When I retire, I'm going to live in Florida, where it's warm all year round.

They never say, when I retire, I'm going to treat people the way they should be treated, the way I've always wanted to be treated. I can't get fired for it. They never say that, but they should, because it's what gives retirement true meaning.

Adelaide looked in the rearview mirror at sleeping Hazel, and to her right at a now-sleeping Don, and realized what she had to do. She had to take up the fight again, but this time on her own terms. She had to start standing up for her own softness and the softness of others. Then she would be a better lover, and a better teacher.

Yes, she would go back to loving and teaching with new purpose, because how else were you going to get more retired people into the world? And isn't that really the point? She needed to gather some strength first, but one day soon she knew she'd be capable of all this and more. Wake up, Adelaide, wake up! she would say to herself on that morning. There are baby quail to feed and snakes to kill, or catch and release beyond the fence. Today is the first day of the rest of your retirement.

9
ARMY OF ONE

Who isn't in the army? When you spend two hours a day playing field hockey, a sport for which you have no talent, a negative capability, in fact, meaning you get in other people's way – isn't that the army? When you're standing out in the mud holding a stick, pretending you know where the ball is and want to smack it, hard, pretending you're just about to start running really fast, pretending you're not thinking about that other girl who got hit in the head with a field hockey ball and had a big black lump on her forehead for two months like a third eye – isn't that the army?

When you spend three hours a week in church, listening to the choir sing off key, feeling dizzy because you had to fast so that you could take communion – a spoonful of wine and a chunk of bread and after that you have to kiss the priest's fat white hand, which smells sweet, sweet and fat and white with dark hairs springing out of the back of it – and then you have to listen to the priest give the deadliest lecture you've ever heard, organized around some anecdote anybody else would be ashamed to tell it's so boring – no, wait, back up, it's not a lecture you're listening to, it's a sermon, because apparently if God's speaking through you, then you don't have to say anything interesting – isn't that the army?

When you have to spend every evening and weekend with the same three people who look like you, and then other days called holidays with them and more people who look like you, when you have to give gifts and receive them or eat turkey, cranberries and stuffing, when you have to remember what day all of those people were born on, when you have to remember their babies' names and the names of their husbands, when you have to keep track of who's dead and who's alive and all of the casualties in between – not that you don't love your family, because you do, you do – but when you have to do all of that without pausing to consider whether you want to or they want to, either, because then the whole thing might fall apart – isn't that the army?

And isn't it the army when you get a job?

And isn't it the army when you buy a house, or a new car, or anything with payments?

And isn't it the army when you get married?

She'd been thinking these things for a long time, quietly, to herself. It would've been unpleasant to say them out loud, and she'd always been a go-along-to-get-along kind of person. Or was it get-along-to-go-along? She wasn't sure, so she just kept her mouth shut. She got a job and a new car and a house with a mortgage, and a partner to share it all with.

And then, when she was in her early thirties – which is late in life for an epiphany, but an epiphany it was – she saw a TV commercial that gave her an idea. A different idea. A different idea and a slogan and eventually, a plan.

It had been a difficult week – everything kept breaking: Partner's glasses, their home security system, the water heater and the washing machine. Looking back on it, that might've been the sign before the sign. In any event, it's how she happened to be sitting in a Laundromat when a young woman came on TV talking about the U.S. Army.

According to the young woman, going into the Army was no longer about joining a team – a team that went around killing other teams– it was about maximizing your full, individual potential. For instance, this young woman had picked a specific career field in the Army and trained specifically for that.

"They really stress education," she said. "And there are a lot more females going into the Army than there used to be."

The ad ended with her waving from a helicopter, and a big booming voice read out the tagline: BECOME AN ARMY OF ONE.

BECOME AN ARMY OF ONE. She looked around the Laundromat to see if the other customers had heard the call – if they were standing frozen in their tracks like her, halfway between terror and ecstasy – but no, they kept right on folding their clothes.

She beat a hasty retreat to the donut shop around the corner. She needed to think. Obviously, if you joined the Army of One – the real Army of One, not the u.s. Army – you had to do it in your own time, in your own way. You couldn't look to others for guidance or reinforcement. I am going to do it tomorrow, she thought, biting decisively into a cruller. Yes, tomorrow.

It would be a radical gesture, some might say an abrupt narrative shift, but she'd been working up to it for some time, she reasoned – her whole life maybe. She knew it wouldn't be easy, because she'd never lived by herself before, no, not for one minute – before Partner she'd had boyfriends and girlfriends and roommates and parents – but it had to be done. Voices don't come to you every day.

She launched her offensive the same day the United States Army invaded Iraq. That caused a certain amount of confusion, but change was in the air. As she was driving over to the North Hollywood Corporate Apartment complex with her car full of stuff, the President was saying on the radio: "The time for diplomacy is over!"

The agent who showed her around explained that the North Hollywood Corporate apartments, while designed for relocating executives, were mostly occupied by local men going through divorces, and child actors and their mothers hoping to break into Hollywood.

"Some of them come and never leave," he said. It wasn't clear if he thought that was a good thing or a bad thing.

She asked him if there were any apartments available right that minute.

"You're looking for you?"

"You could say that."

Her apartment was small, a "studio," and it had a Murphy bed with a big mirror on the underside of it. During the day she folded the bed into the wall and sat on the couch against the opposite wall watching TV. The war was the only thing on. She watched the war on TV every waking moment when she wasn't at work or having harrowing phone conversations with Partner, or watching herself watch the war on TV in the big mirror. She looked terrible, almost as bad as the war.

She was shocked and awed by the broadcast of the United States' "Shock and Awe" bombing campaign. This, not the millennial fireworks, she thought, is the real beginning of the twenty-first century. It's going to suck even worse than the last one. The very idea of the war horrified her, but because of her personal situation, her reactions to specific events were confused. For instance, when U.S. soldiers pulled down the statue of the tyrant Saddam Hussein, she wept for joy. When news commentators wondered aloud what the Iraqis would do with their newfound freedom, she cried out, "God, yes, what will they do?"

Every now and then, she left the room to go weep in the communal hot tub. Weep about her life, not the war, although at the time it was hard to separate the two or know which side was right. The hairy fifty year-old men in the tub with her pretended not to notice, but she could tell they were weeping, too, inside. About their lives, not the war – about how sad it is to be a hairy fifty year-old man in a hot tub. Their wives, who were now divorcing them, had been the only ones standing between them and the truth. Of course, they would find new, younger wives very soon, but they would never be able to shake that feeling.

It's important to look yourself in the face at least once in your life. When she left home, Partner said to her, "You're not as impressive as you think you are." Sitting in the communal hot tub at the North Hollywood Corporate Apartments, she saw how that could be true.

*   *   *

But there was no turning back now. As soon as she joined the Army of One, her entire worldview had shifted. She found she no longer understood the people she'd always understood before, and others whose actions had previously been opaque to her – such as maiden aunts and skydivers – suddenly made sense for the first time. Every song she heard on the radio appalled her.

Sometimes she read the personals to strengthen her resolve:

AFFLUENT MATURE BUSINESS EXEC ISO PETITE FEMALE COMPANION. BE VERY THIN, AFFECTIONATE, SENSUAL, SUPER CLEAN. HAVE A POSITIVE ATTITUDE.

My, my, she clucked, turning the page. Think what a better world it would be if people just left each other alone.

It took her a while to decide on a uniform for her army: tight black jeans, a red Western shirt with gold stitching and metallic gold vinyl boots. For some reason this getup gave her confidence. She didn't wear her uniform much, because the vinyl boots made her feet sweat, but she saw it constantly in her mind's eye.

One day when she was wearing her uniform, the little blonde boy from across the hall asked her if she was a stripper.

"How do you know what a stripper is?"

The little blonde boy winked. "I'm in show business."

She went inside her apartment without answering and taped an inspirational quote to the Murphy bed mirror:

My passionate sense of social justice and social responsibility have always contrasted oddly with my pronounced need for direct contact with other human beings and human communities. I am truly a 'lone traveler' and have never belonged to my country, my home, my friends, or even my immediate family with my whole heart: in the face of all these ties, I have never lost a sense of distance and a need for solitude – feelings which increase with the years.

Now she might not be so impressive, but you couldn't say that about Einstein!

But as she'd suspected, army life was far from easy. When you're in the Army of One, she discovered, you think about death all the time. It's only natural. You think, I better chew slowly, because I could choke and die sitting here at the table in my little corporate apartment. I could be lying dead for three days before anybody found me. Then you think, I'm glad I don't have a cat because my cat might eat me.

But mostly you think about suicide. At first you think your friends and family are going to kill you for starting your own army, like your partner now wants to, but you're surprised to find after a little while they adjust and stop calling all the time. They support the troops, if not the war. That isn't what makes you think about suicide, though, or it is, but not in a negative way. You just start to think, wow, what else can I get away with?

Most people don't really believe their lives belong to them, which is why they go on and on. But staking a claim on your life means that if the least little thing goes wrong, you immediately think of ending it. Why not? It's your life and you don't like how it's going. Like when you get a forty-five dollar parking ticket. Thirty dollars may be reasonable, but forty-five – come on! What kind of a world is that?

In the Army of One, she also discovered, you never cook. You have to save all your energy for combat. If you find yourself cooking, even something like pasta that only takes ten minutes to make, you feel exposed and vulnerable. Anybody could take you out while you're slaving over a hot stove, so instead of cooking, you drink a lot.

You don't sleep much, either. This is because you have night vision. You wake up in the middle of the night and see things very clearly. There is nobody there.

You don't sign up for the Army, though, unless you're ready to commit mind, body and soul. She thought she had the soul part down, but the body part was harder because people were so unco-operative. She didn't understand why she couldn't just roll around for a few days with some nice young guy or girl she met at a party, and do it this way and do it that way without questions being asked. What's wrong with you? What are you so afraid of? Why can't we have breakfast with your friends?

She tried to explain to them that she had to be ready to move at any time. To pick up and go. That her friends were her friends because they never expected to see her for breakfast.

"Oh," said her lovers. "Well then I guess we can't be friends."

To be honest, she was having a little trouble getting her mind around the whole thing, too – which is why, a few months into her stay at the North Hollywood Corporate Apartments, she sought out the Mathematician. She'd heard the hairy fifty-year old men in the hot tub talking about him – apparently the old man was quite famous. Famously reclusive, too – one of the ones who came and never left. Rumor had it that sometimes he went for two weeks without saying more than "thank you" or "large pizza" to a single person.

She suspected the reason the Mathematician could do this was because he loved numbers. She herself didn't have a good feeling about numbers. Numbers reminded her she hadn't paid her credit card bills and was accruing finance charges. Numbers reminded her she was too old to start over. She couldn't see that whole world mathematicians saw where numbers carried on relationships with each other. All of those shapes and patterns that numbers formed were lost on her. She felt sad to be locked out of the world of numbers, but it had never been otherwise. The only number she understood – and that only recently – was the number one. And maybe the number on the other side of one – not two, zero. She wasn't sure that anyone understood two, really. She suspected that what they thought was two was actually one half.

Once you get into fractions, though, things start getting complicated, so she decided to stick to one, at least for the time being. But she still wasn't sure how to do it, exactly, so she snuck up behind the Mathematician in the laundry room. She'd been told he went there sometimes in the middle of the night to work – one of his famous theorems had come to him while staring at a wall of spinning dryers.

"What're you working on?" she asked.

The Mathematician jumped and ran his bony fingers through his thin white hair.

"Who said that?" he asked, looking down the line of dryers.

"I did," she said, tapping his shoulder.

The Mathematician looked relieved to see her.

"I just finished a proof," he said, and handed it to her. It was many pages long.

"Yep," she said, handing it back to him. "It sure looks done."

"I take it you're not a mathematician," he said dryly.

"No," she said. "But I would like to learn more about numbers."

As luck would have it, the Mathematician was a number theorist. His area of specialty was absolute primes – the lone wolves of numbers. A prime is a number that can't be divided by any other number except the number one, he explained to her. An absolute prime is a number that remains prime even upon a re-ordering of its digits.

"So when I'm thirty-seven," she said, "I will be prime?"

"Absolute prime," the Mathematician snapped, turning back to the dryers.

That night she had a dream about numbers.

"You can't go backwards from two to one," Partner was telling her, as if life were a giant hopscotch game. "You can only go forward to three."

That was why Partner left her, because Partner wanted to have a baby and she wasn't sure. Wait, no, she left Partner.

"Ever think maybe you're the one going backward?" she said in the dream. "From one to one-half to a third?"

"See?" Partner said. "You were always selfish."

A few days later, she was fortunate to spot the Mathematician slip out of his apartment carrying a bag of clothes. Well, okay, she'd been standing outside his door all morning, but in any event she was able to accompany him the short distance to the onsite dry cleaners. As far as she knew, the Mathematician was the only one in the complex who availed himself of this service – which again, was intended for relocating executives.

"Have you ever had a partner or a baby?" she asked, falling into step beside him. The Mathematician looked annoyed.

"Both," he said, "but neither one talks to me now."

"Why not?"

"They said I was selfish," the Mathematician said, pushing open the door to the dry cleaners. "Now leave me alone."

Is it selfish to believe the world would be a better place if people spent a little more time by themselves? she wondered, as she wended her way back to her room. Because it seemed to her that if you were happily by yourself – that is to say, alone on purpose – you wouldn't have either the inclination or the opportunity to hurt other people. Oh you can always get to people, but if you're actively trying not to get to them, there's no way you can do the same amount of damage. It's the Law of Averages. She didn't know what that meant exactly, but it sounded mathematical and pure.

When you're alone you also have time to think about what people are doing wrong and what they're doing right – to you and to each other – and you have time to do math and write things and envision a better world. Plus if you don't see people for a long time, it's easier to be delighted when you do see them. You might even do something nice for them, like mow their lawn. You certainly wouldn't torture them, or rape their sixteen-year old daughter, or blow a big hole in the side of their house, the way u.s. soldiers were doing in Iraq.

There are plenty of folks who should be in the Army of One, she decided, but never find the courage to enlist. Instead, they wait around to be drafted, resenting their friends and families for taking up so much of their time, and accumulating a vast porn collection or a novel in a drawer. She'd been one of those people. They're the ones who are strangely chipper at funerals. They're also the ones who drive too fast, and cheat at ping-pong. It's a pity they can't just get called up, because the Army of One would straighten them out.

Her mother was of the opinion that females didn't belong in the Army.

"I just don't want you to be lonely, darling," she said.

"I would rather be lonely than with someone who doesn't appreciate me," she responded, thinking it over. "Someone I have to be careful not to upset. Someone who calls me 'dippy.' Someone who runs through my hard-earned money. Someone who starts drinking at ten am." She'd just described each of her mother's five husbands, one of whom was her father.

"Easy," her mother said. "You don't want to end up a selfish old bitch, either."

The night after she escorted the Mathematician to the dry cleaners, she dreamed that she was running down the street screaming and crying because somebody had stolen her dinner. Even though it had only taken her ten minutes to make, that just felt like the last straw, you know? Then, out of nowhere, Partner appeared and said, "Here, you can have my dinner." She knew it was a dream as she was dreaming it, because that would never happen in real life. Not now. Partner had stopped calling in the middle of the night, waking her from dreams of Partner. From here on out, she was on her own.

Of course, like any soldier, she constantly thought about deserting, usually after she had sex, or hugged a friend's child, or received a complete skin care system or a thigh reducer in the mail from her mother, who had a little home shopping problem. What battle, what war is more important than the smell and the touch and the feel of another person?

Unable to answer that question, one morning she slipped out of bed at dawn and shouldered her pack with a heavy heart. "Goodbye," she said softly to the person still sleeping, but the still sleeping person didn't reply. And so, putting one gold stripper boot in front of the other, she began the long march back to Base. As she marched, she stared at the horizon, trying to see where she was headed, but it was hazy, a shifting landscape. At first she thought she glimpsed a blacktop highway in the distance, one she could whiz along forever, but when she looked again, she saw only dirt roads and washed-out bridges and abandoned cars. Not long after, she spotted a traveling circus, which made her smile and quicken her pace, but when she rounded the corner it was gone. Many hours into her march, she saw another solitary figure on the trail way ahead of her and her heart skipped a beat –if only she could catch up! Would she always walk this path alone?

But while she hadn't worked out the specifics yet, she still thought her idea was sound. There are 480,000 men and women in the United States Army. Imagine if they really were, each of them, an Army of One.

10
A IS FOR ANARCHY

To the Members of the Panorama Hills Book Club:

It is with great sadness that I tender my letter of resignation. Great sadness, and, okay, the tiniest bit of anger. Not towards anyone in particular, but towards our Book Club as a collective. Frankly, ladies, I have come to believe you are, for want of a better word, close-minded. What other possible conclusion could I come to, given your refusal to read Peter Marshall's *Demanding the Impossible: A History of Anarchism*, George Woodcock's *Anarchism*, or indeed, any book having anything to do with anarchism at all? Granted, the Marshall was seven hundred pages, the Woodcock four hundred seventy, and we are all busy wives and mothers, but anarchism has a long and involved history. And how to explain your voting this month against *Anarchism: A Very Short Introduction* as our next selection?

Believe me, in the first, heady days of the Book Club, I harbored no such suspicions. On the contrary, those nights of laughter, of tears and confession, all of us sitting in a tight circle in Elaine's living room (which has the exact same layout as my living room, only reversed) – those memories I will always cherish! Why, we asked, and what for? And who says? And did the granite top counter come with this model or was it extra (although we saved that sort of question for bathroom break)? It wasn't just our Book Club that was new then, it was Panorama Hills itself – or no, I guess Panorama Hills has been around for a few decades but with so many houses going up last year it felt like a whole new town. And didn't we share family photos? And didn't we share paint swatches? And didn't we share landscaping services? And didn't we cheer for the new trees through the picture window, waving their bare little arms?

And you were all so understanding about Justin – the trouble Rick and I've had with him. Really, so understanding. Brandon was fine with the move, he's a happy kid – so far, anyway. Brandon would be fine if we moved to Baghdad. But Justin – you would've thought we HAD moved to Baghdad, the way he carried on. No, a skateboard can't get you across the freeway, but that was sort of the point, from his father's and my perspective. A new beginning in California, for all of us, as a family. A new house, a new lawn and new friends like you who were interested in literature and ideas.

But it was actually Justin who made me start to question things, the last time he and I were down at the Sheriff's Station. Rick, as you know, refuses to come with me anymore when Justin gets picked up. He says he should just do time.

"What were you doing?" I asked Justin.

"Taking a walk," he said.

"Sheriffs don't pick you up for taking a walk."

"Sure they do. It's called loitering."

"You were out after curfew."

"Curfew is ten o'clock. I never go to bed before midnight."

"Justin, you're only fifteen."

And then Justin said something that really got to me, because I've always tried to treat my boys with respect. Even before they could talk, I listened to them. As you all know, I've tried to be that kind of mother.

What he said was, "Am I not a human being?"

Oh sure, that was the message of To Kill a Mockingbird and Brave New World and even Animal Farm, as we all decided. But to have your own son look you in the eye in the lobby of the Sheriff's Station and say exactly the same thing –

"Of course you are, darling!" I cried, as any mother would.

"Then why can't I take a walk after ten o'clock? Why don't I have freedom of association with my friends? Why am I treated like a criminal where I live and go to school?"

I know what you're all thinking – to be honest, I was thinking it, too, at that moment, and I said it out loud, because it was my duty as a mother to do so.

"Justin, you dress all in black, and you have a mohawk and a tattoo of two weird guys on your arm. Your friends never emerge from their hooded sweatshirts long enough for us to tell them apart, and none of you ever looks an adult in the eye. Is it because you're on drugs? Last month when I held the Book Club at our home my friends thought you were a burglar! You're a good boy, you're a reader and a dreamer and you're kind to your little brother, but I don't know why you can't wear pastels once in a while or even just primary colors!"

So he said what he was thinking right back, which I was happy about – honest, immediate communication between a mother and a teenage son, that's a rare thing these days – until I heard what he was saying. Then I grabbed his arm and hustled him out of the Sheriff's Station and told him to wait till we got to the car, because what he was saying was this: neither he nor any of his friends are "on drugs," which is not to say they don't do them from time to time; he doesn't look adults in the eye because he doesn't feel like being condescended to; the two weird guys on his arm are Sacco and Vanzetti, a pair of Italian anarchists who got the electric chair in Boston in the nineteen twenties; and Justin is an anarchist, too.

"Okay," I said, pulling out onto the Old Road. Cars were honking and whizzing by but I had to go slow because I had to think. I turned onto that new road behind the supermarket to get back to our place – that new, new road, I don't think most people even know it's there yet. I only just discovered it on one of my rambles with Brandon. We sometimes get lost coming home from the box stores, it's easy to lose track when I'm singing along to a Raffi song or answering a question about coyotes, one of those three or four-part questions Brandon likes to dream up – especially since the new roads aren't marked, or if they are, the names don't mean anything yet. To be honest, it's sort of nice to get lost that way, it's like being on the edge of every place you've ever been, but an edge that goes on and on until it becomes the place itself. It's a dreamy, open-ended sort of experience, so long as it doesn't go on too long, so long as you get shot back out onto the Old Road after a while, back to the box stores, although to be honest that feels a little unreal too when you first come to it, that forest of neon signs blaring at you out of nowhere, but I always take comfort in the fact that there are other people around again, if only in their cars.

But this time I took the new road because I didn't want anyone to see us having this conversation, if only in our car. It felt like a very dangerous conversation, you can understand that, a very dangerous conversation for a mother to be having with her son.

"Are you in contact with Al Qaeda?" I finally asked, and I couldn't believe the words were coming out of my mouth, but such is parenting a teenager in today's world and let no one say I did not meet the challenge.

"MOM," Justin groaned. "I'm not a terrorist, I'm an anarchist!"

"What's the difference?" I said. "Don't anarchists plant bombs? Isn't that what your friends Sacco and Vanzetti did?"

"Some anarchists plant bombs, but that's not the point of anarchism. And no, Sacco and Vanzetti "DIDN'T." They were "INNOCENT."

"Well, if they were innocent, why did they go to the electric chair?"

Justin sighed and closed his eyes, and I felt the window of conversational opportunity closing, fast, and I stuck my foot out to stop it.

"What is anarchism, honey? Honestly, I don't really know."

He looked over at me suspiciously, but I could see a glimmer of hope in his eyes.

"Tell me, kiddo. I promise I won't tell Dad."

Well, that opened the floodgates, and Justin started prattling on about self-organizing collectives and no need for the State and the right of every human being to represent his or her own best interests and spontaneous association and temporary autonomous zones and lively social feeling and a bunch of authors I'd never heard of before, although I know them now – Kropotkin and Proudhoun and Bakhunin and Emma Goldman and David

Graeber and Hakim Bey – and how anarchism doesn't need bombs or a revolution because it can happen right here, right now, wherever and whenever you are, because it's a way of being and a way of thinking and a way of respecting your fellow human beings.

And I was smiling and nodding with tears in my eyes, because it was like having the old Justin back – you can understand that, right? Justin when he was Brandon's age, so curious and alive and loving. And I thought, well, there must be something to this anarchism if it's got Justin so revved up, so I asked him to recommend me some books and he looked at me and sighed again, but it was a nice look and a sort-of-hopeful sigh. Then the minivan started to act up the way it's been doing lately, jerking and popping and then conking out for good. While I was trying to start it up again Justin looked around and asked, "Where are we, anyway?" and I looked around and had no idea.

As you all know, I'm an avid reader, so over the next couple of weeks I read all of the books Justin had recommended to me and a few more besides, and believe me, they really changed my outlook on things. What I started to see was not so much what was wrong with everything (which is how people think anarchists look at the world) but what was right with everything. How close we were, even – no, especially – here in Panorama Hills, to a kind of anarcho-socialist utopia, with just a little bit of tweaking.

For instance, one day I stopped off at Juicy Juicy Juice with Brandon on the way to an Up with Kids! birthday party one of his friends was having. I'd never been to a Juicy Juicy Juice before, but Brandon had to pee. He had to pee about ten minutes after we left Juicy Juicy Juice, too, so maybe it wasn't the wisest pit stop. But anyway, we walked in the door and a bunch of teenagers in brightly colored t-shirts started shouting "Hello!" "Hi!" "Hi!" "Hello!" at us, which kind of took me aback, because that's not what teenagers are usually shouting – at me or anybody. So I took a closer look at their twinkling braces and their spotty faces and their firm flesh and just the, you know, dumb goodwill they were emanating and thought to myself, this looks like a self-organizing collective if I've ever seen one!

Now obviously Juicy Juicy Juice is not a self-organizing collective, but how much would it take to make them one, I wondered, as I wound my way up through the hills. Somehow I'd wondered all the way back down to Juicy Juicy Juice again before I realized what was happening, so it was back up the hill and over the top this time and down through Villa Romana, a brand new development in the Mediterranean Style – you should see the square footage on those houses – and out onto a new part of the Old Road I'd never seen before. And there, in the middle of a whole other set of box stores, Brandon and I finally located the Up With Kids! Party Center.

When we got there, the party was already in full swing. Fifty kids jumping up and down and screaming their heads off in rubber bounce houses made to look like castles and dragons – so much energy, so much power, I thought, and such a waste! I was really grappling with the big questions that afternoon, as I watched my son's pale little face disappear and reappear and disappear again through the plastic bounce house window. There was too much noise to do more than wave and smile at the other parents, but I don't know what I would've said to them anyway, given the mood I was in. "Don't you see we've put our children in cages?" is what I really wanted to say. "Soft, pillowy cages? Is this freedom? Is this life? Is this really Up With Kids?"

But what was the point? No one could hear me.

I couldn't contain myself, though, when they ushered us into the birthday cake room and lifted the birthday boy up onto a giant inflatable throne. "No Gods, No Masters!" I shouted, just as Brandon – appropriately, I thought – splattered his Juicy Juicy Juice at the birthday king's feet.

And that's when – the next day – I came to you with my book selection nominations. I was in such a ferment, you see, and I wanted to share my excitement with all of you. Like when Elaine read the expose of the Atkins Diet, or Lisa read that child abuse memoir, I wanted to know what you thought, and I wanted you to help me understand what I thought. What's more, I felt sure that you could. And while of course I realize *Pride and Prejudice* is a timeless classic and we've agreed to focus on Great Literature this year, I can't see why it trumped my urgent – no, emergency nominations! I can only think that the turmoil I was going through right then must have frightened you, perhaps you were afraid that reading about anarchism might upend your world too, and in that there is some small compensation.

A few days later, I had a conversation with Rick, because this is the kind of change-in-life's-direction you need to share with your husband.

"I don't understand," he said. "You want to live on a commune?"

"I feel like we already do live on a commune in some ways," I said. "It's really the same concept isn't it, gated community?"

Rick snorted. "Sure, except nobody shares anything and everyone else is richer than we are. I'm barely making the payments here, babe."

"I'm sure my book club would take up a collection for us, if need be."

"Oh you are, are you," he said with a sour look. I might as well come out and say it now, Rick loves literature – we met in a class on Melville – but he's not a big fan of the Panorama Hills Book Club, not since Elaine knocked over his ship in a bottle when I hosted and broke it.

"Anyway, anarchism's bigger than communes," I said, struggling to explain. "It's like – love. Like if the world were organized according to the love principle, instead of the profit motive."

"So those punks smashing up the Queequeg's in Seattle – that was the love principle?"

"Well, that's not how I would've gone about it, but they were trying to call attention to the violence of the corporation, and the power it has over our lives. They didn't hurt anyone."

"They hurt Queequeg."

"Queequeg is not a person. Okay, he's a character in Moby Dick, but that's not what we're talking about here."

Rick sighed and rubbed his eyes, the way he's been doing ever since we moved to Panorama Hills. He and Justin are always sighing these days, only at different times.

"The minivan is acting up, honey," I said, to keep the conversation going. "I think I should take it in."

Rick didn't say anything, just sat there with his hand over his eyes.

"It keeps conking out, and the brakes are going, I think. I have to pump them really hard."

Rick was still sitting there with his hand over his eyes, but all of a sudden his shoulders were shaking.

"Honey?" I said.

"I can't do it," he sobbed.

"Can't do what?"

"I can't do any of it. We're broke."

"Honey!" I said, putting my arms around him. My Rick is not a crybaby, ladies, so I knew something was terribly wrong.

"We have to move," he said, after a moment, wiping the tears away and sitting up.

"Have to move?" my lips echoed, but no sound came out.

"Yes, that's it," Rick said, with a faraway look in his eyes. "We'll just have to move."

Well, ladies, I am not a quitter, present circumstances excepted, and I was not about to just move out of Panorama Hills. So that night I sat down with other non-working members of the family and explained the situation.

"Right on!" Justin whooped. "Let's move!"

I gave him a withering look. "And since when do you think money should determine the course of social relations?"

He shrugged and crossed his arms. "What do you want me to do?"

"How about get a job? After school."

Justin's jaw dropped.

"What do you want me to do, Mom?" Brandon piped up. "You want me to get a job, too?"

"You're too little, baby," I said, patting his hand. "But you could stop asking me to go to Juicy Juicy Juice all the time."

Brandon's jaw dropped, too. I was starting to enjoy myself.

"I'm going to get a job," I said. "Part-time. While you're in school."

"What kind of job?" Justin asked suspiciously.

"I don't know. I'll find something."

Justin stroked the eight to ten darling little hairs on his chin, staring into the distance. "Vanzetti had a fish cart. Every morning he went to the dock and loaded it up. Every evening he came home with one fish left for dinner."

"Fish cart's a start," I said. "You'd be your own boss. Make your own hours."

Justin nodded, still stroking his chin. "But where will I get the fish?"

"Maybe you could sell something else."

He frowned. "And then we just give the money to Dad?"

"No, then I think we hold a meeting to decide what to do with it, right?"

Justin smiled for the first time since we got to Panorama Hills – honestly, the first time – and removed his feet from the kitchen table without being told.

"Count me in!" he said, standing up.

Oh, Ladies, I can't tell you what it's like to witness the moment your boy becomes a man!

The next day I went looking for work. I started at the Jupiter dealership because I'd heard they made a point of being honest and sincere with their customers. I'd heard Jupiter held seminars for new car owners where they could learn all about how their cars worked and how to take care of them. I'd even heard there were Jupiter reunions once a year, an opportunity for Jupiter drivers from all over the country to bond over their experiences. I think I heard all of that from a Jupiter commercial, but who cares, if it's true?

So I walked into the dealership – they call it a retail facility – and was standing there staring at a shiny new Jupiter when I heard a voice behind me, such a kind voice, say, "Has anyone helped you today?"

I almost expected to see an angel when I turned around, but what I saw was the next best thing, a retail consultant with the name tag Dan Villard and the most honest face I'd ever looked into – a little pouchy, maybe, but honest pouches, if you know what I mean.

So I said, "Yes, some people have helped me today, like the lady at the supermarket who got my cart untangled, but others have not been so helpful, like the credit card customer service representative I spoke to on the phone this morning."

"I know exactly how you feel," Dan said, patting my shoulder, and I actually believed him. I hadn't been expecting to form a spontaneous association with a Jupiter retail consultant, but I was willing to go with it. He motioned me upstairs and we sat at his desk for a long time overlooking the showroom and just talked, you know? Sure, we were talking about Jupiters – especially the L-Series and all of the awards it's won for fuel efficiency and storage space – but we were talking about much more than Jupiters. We were talking about a code of ethics. It's a little hard to explain, but the shorthand version is this: if everybody in the world behaved according to Jupiter values, there wouldn't be any sexism or racism or war or capitalism even. You would never look around the Up With Kids! Party Center and think, why doesn't anyone ever rise to the occasion? In a Jupiter world, everyone would rise to the occasion.

It was mostly me saying these things, but Dan agreed, and he was able to supply all of the particulars I was missing. He even pulled out the Jupiter Values Statement and showed it to me. One value impressed me so much, I copied it down in my datebook. It was entitled Trust and Respect for the Individual:

We have nothing of greater value than our people! We believe that demonstrating respect for the uniqueness of every individual builds a team of confident, creative members possessing a high degree of initiative, self-respect and self-discipline.

"Why, that's anarchy in action!" I said, and Dan let out a belly laugh and asked me what I was driving right now. So I told him all about the minivan and how it was going to die any minute, I could feel it, especially on the hills. My eyes started to tear up and my voice got quavery, what with all that was going on, but Dan told me not to worry, it would be okay.

"Why don't we take a walk out onto the lot?" he said. "It's really nice this time of day."

And he was right, it was just starting to get dark and the Jupiters were kind of glowing in the sun, which was setting right over the retail facility. With the light like that, it was as if we were walking into a whole new world, Dan and I, and I could feel the spirits of thousands, maybe millions of satisfied Jupiter owners all around us, like a whole new species. Aliens, maybe, but the good kind of aliens who are thousands of light years ahead of us on the road to understanding.

"How beautiful!" I said, spinning around to take it all in.

"So how about it?" Dan said. "You want to trade in that old minivan for a new Jupiter?"

"Goodness no!" I said, coming to a stop. "We can't even afford to make the repairs! No, I'm here to apply for a job!"

Dan looked at me for a long moment with his sad pouchy eyes and then looked down at his watch and shook his head, like he wished he could just give me a new car and end all my troubles right there and then.

"I'll get you an application," he said. "You can fill it out at home."

When I left the Jupiter retail facility I was on top of the world, it felt like all of those red white and blue balloons and banners flapping in the wind were for me, like they were saying "You can get a job!" and "You don't have to leave Panorama Hills!" and "Emma Goldman would be proud!" I picked Brandon up from school and he showed me the illustration he'd made for his letter of the alphabet: a stick figure drawing of him and me and his father and brother and his teacher and a man with pink hair he called a "hair stylist" and three hooded boys, his brother's friends – all of us holding hands – and underneath, the inscription "A IS FOR ANARCHY."

I hugged him hard and told him that art is very important. "I'll put this up on the fridge, baby," I said, "and it will give us courage to face the day."

So you see, Ladies, though I'm resigning from the Panorama Hills Book Club, I still believe in art and the power of ideas and the potential of collectivity, and I hope one day you'll take all of those things a little more seriously. I hope one day soon you'll get to feel what I felt as Brandon and I started up the new road towards home and spotted a lone figure in a black raincoat in the distance, silhouetted against the tiny, bare-armed trees, pushing some contraption along the sidewalk. At first I thought it was a stroller, naturally, but then I realized it was an ice cream cart! I caught up to it on the other side of the crest and tried to stop, but that just so happened to be the moment the brakes on the minivan gave out completely. No matter, Justin saw us waving, Brandon and I, as we sailed by, and we saw him wave back, and maybe that was all any of us needed to continue.

FINIS

ACKNOWLEDGEMENTS

My deep and abiding thanks to Peter Gadol, editor, friend and mentor.

Thanks also to Rebecca Baron, Fiona Jack, Deborah Lowe, Tracy McNulty, Maggie Nelson, Barbara Moroncini, Steve Erickson, Susan Simpson and Christine Wertheim, for lending their insight and encouragement to this project, and to my colleagues and students at CalArts, for continued inspiration.

Thank you to my family, especially my mother and father, for their love and support. And to Ken, fellow seeker.

An earlier version of "Bunker Mentality" appeared in *Plum Ruby Review*

An earlier version of "Alien Encounter" appeared in *Black Clock*

An earlier version of "Warming the World" was published in *Black Clock* under the title "Responsible Hedonism"